Five Go Down To The Sea

Enid Blyton

THE FAMOUS FIVE

Five Go Down To The Sea

Hodder
Children's
Books

A division of Hachette Children's Books

Enid Blyton ® Famous Five ® Copyright © 2010 Chorion Rights Ltd
All rights reserved
'Foreword' copyright Sophie Smallwood 2010

First published in Great Britain in 1953 by Hodder and Stoughton

This revised edition first published in 2010 by Hodder Children's Books

With thanks to Rachel Elliot

The right of Enid Blyton to be identified as the Author of
the Work has been asserted by her in accordance with the
Copyright, Designs and Patents Act 1988.

4

A Catalogue record for this book is available from the British Library

ISBN 978 0 340 93170 7

Typeset by Avon DataSet Ltd, Bidford-on-Avon, Warwickshire

Printed and bound in Great Britain by Clays Ltd, St Ives plc

The paper and board used in this paperback by Hodder Children's Books
are natural recyclable products made from wood grown in sustainable
forests. The manufacturing processes conform to the environmental
regulations of the country of origin.

Hodder Children's Books
a division of Hachette Children's Books
338 Euston Road, London NW1 3BH
An Hachette UK company
www.hachette.co.uk

Contents

1 *The holiday begins*

'Oh no! I've got a puncture!' said Dick. 'My tyre's going flat. Worst time it could possibly happen!'

Julian glanced down at Dick's back tyre. Then he looked at his watch.

'You've just got time to pump it up and hope for the best,' he said. 'We've got seven minutes before the train goes.'

Dick jumped off and took his pump. The others got off their bikes, too, and stood around, watching to see if the tyre blew up well or not.

They were on their way to Kirrin Station to catch the train, bikes and all. Their luggage had gone on in advance, and they thought they had left plenty of time to ride to the station, get their bikes labelled and put in the luggage van, and catch the train comfortably.

'We *can't* miss the train!' said George, putting on her best scowl.

She always hated it when things went wrong.

'We can. Easiest thing in the world!' said Julian, grinning at George's fierce face. 'What do *you* say, Timmy?'

Timmy barked sharply, as if to say he agreed. He licked George's hand and she patted him. The scowl left her face as she saw Dick's tyre coming up well. They'd just make it! Dick felt his tyre, gave a sigh of relief, and put his pump back in its place.

'Phew! That was hot work,' he said, mounting his bike. 'Hope it'll last till we get to the station. I was afraid you'd have to go without me.'

'Oh, *no*,' said Anne. 'We'd have caught the next train. Come on, Timmy!'

The four cousins and Timmy the dog raced on towards the station. They cycled into the station yard just as the signal went up to show the train was due. The station assistant came towards them, his big round face red and smiling.

'I sent your luggage off for you,' he said. 'Not much between you – just one small trunk!'

'Well, we don't wear much on holidays,' said Julian. 'Can you label our bikes quickly for us? I see the train's due.'

The station assistant began to label the four

bikes. He didn't hurry. He wouldn't let the train go off again till he'd done his job, that was certain. There it was now, coming around the bend.

'You going off to Cornwall, I see?' said the station assistant. 'And to Tremannon, too. You want to be careful of swimming there. That's a fierce coast and a hungry sea.'

'Oh, do you know it?' said Anne, surprised. 'Is it a nice place?'

'Nice? Well, I don't know about that,' said the station assistant, raising his voice as the train came rumbling in. 'I used to go out in my uncle's fishing boat all around there, and it's wild and lonely. I wouldn't have thought it was much of a place for a holiday – no pier, no ice-cream sellers, no shows, no cinema, no—'

'Good,' said Julian. 'We can do without all those, thanks. We want to swim, and hire a boat, and fish, and bike all around. That's *our* kind of holiday!'

'Woof!' said Timmy, wagging his tail.

'Yes, and yours too,' said George, rubbing his big head. 'Come on, we'd better get onto the train.'

'I'll see to your bikes,' said the station assistant.

'Have a good holiday, and if you see my uncle tell him you know me. His name's the same as mine, John Polpenny.'

' "By Tre, Pol and Pen, you may know the Cornishmen",' quoted Julian, getting into a carriage with the others. 'Thanks, Mr Polpenny. We'll look up your uncle if we can!'

They each took a seat, and Timmy went to the door, put his feet up on the ledge and his nose out of the window. He wanted to stand like that all the way! He loved the rush of air past his nose.

'Timmy, come down,' said George.

Timmy took no notice. He was happy. It was holidays again, and he was with everybody he loved. They were going away together. There might be rabbits to chase. Timmy had never yet caught a rabbit, but he went on hoping!

'Now, we're off again!' said Julian, settling into his seat. 'I love the beginnings of a holiday, getting ready, looking at maps, planning how to get there, and then at last setting off!'

'On a lovely sunny day like this!' said Anne. 'George, how did your mum hear about Tremannon Farm?'

'Well, it was Dad who heard about it, really,'

said George. 'You know Dad's got a lot of scientist friends who like to go off to lonely places and work out all kinds of ideas in peace and quiet. Well, one of them went to Tremannon Farm because he heard it was one of the quietest places in the country. Dad said his friend went there all skin and bone and came back as fat as a Christmas goose, and Mum said that sounded *just* the place for us to go these holidays!'

'She's right!' said Dick. 'I feel a bit skin-and-bonish myself after slaving at school for three months. I could do with fattening up!'

They all laughed. 'You may *feel* skin-and-bonish, but you don't look it,' said Julian. 'You want a bit of exercise to take your fat off. We'll get it, too. We'll walk and bike and swim and climb . . .'

'And eat,' said George. 'Timmy, you have to be polite to farm dogs, or you'll have a bad time.'

'And you have to remember that when you go out to play, you'll have to ask the other dogs' permission before you can chase their rabbits,' said Dick solemnly.

Timmy thumped his tail against Dick's knees and opened his mouth to let his tongue hang out.

He looked exactly as if he were laughing.

'That's right. Grin at my jokes,' said Dick. 'I'm glad you're coming, Tim, it'd be awful without you.'

'He always *has* come with us, on every holiday,' said George. 'And he's shared in every single adventure we've ever had.'

'Well, he might share in one this time, too,' said Julian. 'You never know.'

'I'm not going to have any adventures this time,' said Anne in a firm voice. 'I just want a holiday, nothing more. Let's have a really good time, and not go on looking for anything strange or mysterious or adventurous.'

'Right,' said Julian. 'Adventures are *off* this time. Definitely off. And if anything does turn up, we ignore it and walk off. Is that agreed?'

'Yes,' said Anne.

'All right,' said George, doubtfully.

'Fine,' said Dick.

Julian looked surprised. 'You're a boring lot. Well, I'll go along with it, if you're all agreed. Even if we find ourselves right in the very middle of Who Knows What, we say "No, thanks" and walk away. That's agreed.'

'Well,' began George, 'I'm not sure if—'

But what she wasn't sure about nobody knew because Timmy chose that moment to fall off the seat. He yelped as he hit the floor with a bang, and immediately went back to his post at the window, putting his head right out.

'We'll have to get him in and shut the windows,' said George. 'He might get something in his eye.'

'No, I'm not going to cook in this hot carriage with all the windows shut, not even for the sake of Timmy's eyes,' said Julian, firmly. 'If you can't make him obey you and come inside, he can just get something in his eye.'

However, the problem was solved very quickly because at that moment the train gave an unearthly shriek and disappeared headlong into utter blackness. Timmy, astounded, fell back into the carriage and tried to get on to George's knee, terrified.

'Don't be a baby, Timmy,' said George. 'It's only a tunnel! Ju, pull him off me. It's too hot to try and nurse a heavy dog like Timmy. Stop it, Timmy, I tell you it's only a *tunnel*!'

The journey seemed very long. The carriage was so hot, and they had to change twice. Timmy panted loudly and hung his tongue out; George begged the station assistants for water at each changing place.

They had their lunch with them, but somehow they weren't hungry. They got dirtier and dirtier, and thirstier and thirstier, for they very quickly drank the orangeade they had brought with them.

'Phew!' said Julian, fanning himself with a magazine. 'I wish I could have a swim. Timmy, don't pant all over me. You make me feel even hotter.'

'What time do we get there?' asked Anne.

'Well, we have to get out at Polwilly Halt,' said Julian. 'That's the nearest place to Tremannon Farm. We bike from there. With luck, we should be there by tea-time.'

'We ought to have brought masses more to drink,' said Dick. 'I feel like a man who's been lost in a sun-scorched desert for weeks.'

They were all extremely glad when they at last arrived at Polwilly Halt. At first they didn't think it was a stop, but it was. It was nothing but a tiny wooden platform built beside the railway. The children sat and waited. They hadn't even seen the little wooden platform or the small sign that said 'Polwilly Halt'.

The sound of impatient feet came along the little platform. The guard's perspiring face appeared at the window.

'Well? Didn't you want to get out here? You going to sit there all day?'

'Oh! Is this Polwilly?' said Julian, leaping up. 'Sorry. We didn't know it was a stop. We'll be out in a second.'

The train started off almost before they had banged the door. They stood there on the funny little platform, all alone except for their four bikes at the other end. The little place seemed lonely and lost, set in the midst of rolling fields and rounded hills. Not a building was in sight!

But not far off to the west George's sharp eyes saw something lovely. She pulled Julian's arm. 'Look, the sea! Over there, between the hills, in the dip. Can you see it? I'm sure it's the sea. What an amazing blue.'

'It's always that gorgeous blue on the Cornish coast,' said Dick. 'Oh, I feel better when I see that. Come on, let's get our bikes and find our way to Tremannon Farm. If I don't get something to drink soon I'll hang my tongue out, like Timmy.'

They went to get their bikes. Dick felt his back tyre. It was a bit soft, but not too bad. He could easily pump it up again.

'How far is it to Tremannon Farm?' he asked.

Julian looked at his notes. '"Get out at Polwilly Halt. Then bike four miles to Tremannon Farm, along narrow lanes. Tremannon Village is about one mile before you get to the farm." Not too bad. We could get some lemonade, or even an ice-cream, in the village.'

'Woof, woof,' said Timmy, who knew the word ice-cream very well indeed.

'Poor Tim!' said Anne. 'He'll be so hot running beside our bikes. We'd better go slowly.'

'Well, if you think I'm going to race along, you can think again,' said Dick. 'I'll go as slowly as you like, Anne!'

They set off with Timmy down a funny little lane, deep-set between high hedges. They went slowly for Timmy's sake. He panted along valiantly. He'd never give up as long as he was with the four children.

It was about five o'clock and a very lovely

evening. They met nobody at all, not even a tractor. It was even too hot for the birds to sing. No wind blew. There seemed a strange silence and loneliness everywhere.

Julian looked back at the other three with a grin. 'Adventure's in the air! I feel it. We're all set for adventure! But we'll turn our backs on it and say: "Go away!" That's agreed!'

2 *Tremannon Farm*

It was a lovely ride to Tremannon Farm. Poppies blew by the wayside in hundreds, and honeysuckle threw its scent out from the hedges as they passed. The corn stood high in the fields, touched with gold already, and splashed with the scarlet of the poppies.

They came to Tremannon Village at last. It was really nothing but a winding street, set with a few shops and houses, and beyond that, straggling out, were other houses. Farther off, set in the hills, were a few farmhouses, their grey stone walls gleaming in the sun.

The four children found the general store and went in.

'Any ice-cream?' said Julian hopefully.

But there was none. What a disappointment! There was orangeade and lemonade, however, quite cool through being kept down in the cellar of the store.

'Are you the people that Mrs Penruthlan is having in?' said the village shopkeeper. 'She's expecting you. Foreigners, aren't you?'

'Well, not exactly,' said Julian, remembering that to many Cornish people anyone was a foreigner who didn't belong to Cornwall. 'My mum had a great-aunt who lived in Cornwall all her life. So we're not *exactly* "foreigners", are we?'

'You're foreigners all right,' said the shopkeeper, looking at Julian with bird-like eyes. 'Your talk is foreign-like, too. Like that man Mrs Penruthlan had before. We reckoned he was mad, although he was harmless enough.'

'Really?' said Julian, pouring himself out a third lemonade. 'Well, he was a scientist, and if you're going to be a really *good* one you have to be a bit mad, you know. At least, so I've heard. Oh, this lemonade is good. Can I have another bottle, please?'

The woman suddenly laughed, sounding just like an amused hen. 'Well, well, Marty Penruthlan's got a lovely meal ready for you, but it seems like you won't be able to eat a thing, not with all that lemonade splashing about in your innards!'

'Don't say you can hear the splashing,' said Julian. 'Very bad manners, that! Foreigners' manners, I'm sure. Well, how much do we owe you? That was really good lemonade.'

He paid the bill and they all mounted their bikes once more, having been given minute directions as to how to get to the farm. Timmy set off with them, feeling much refreshed, having drunk steadily for four minutes without stopping.

'I think you've had enough water to fill a horse-trough, Timmy,' Julian told him. 'If this weather holds we're going to get really brown!'

It was an uphill ride to Tremannon Farm, but they got there at last. As they cycled through the open gates, a fusillade of barks greeted them, and four large dogs came flying to meet them. Timmy put up his hackles at once and growled warningly. He went completely stiff, and stood there glaring.

A woman came out behind the dogs, her face one large smile. 'Now, Ben; now, Bouncer! Here, Nellie, here! Bad dog, Willy! It's all right, children, that's their way of saying "Welcome to Tremannon Farm!"'

The dogs now stood in a ring around the four

children, their tongues out, three collies and one small black Scottie. Timmy eyed them one by one. George had her hand on his collar, just in case he should feel foolhardy all of a sudden and imagine he could take on all four dogs single-handed.

But he didn't. He behaved like a perfect gentleman! His tail wagged politely, and his hackles went down. The little Scottie ran up to him and sniffed his nose. Timmy sniffed back, his tail wagging more vigorously.

Then the three sheepdogs ran up, beautiful collies with plumy tails, and the children heaved sighs of relief to see that the farm dogs evidently weren't going to regard Timmy as a 'foreigner'!

'They're all right now,' said Mrs Penruthlan. 'They've introduced themselves to one another. Now come along with me. You must be tired and dirty – and hungry and thirsty. I've got tea waiting for you.'

She didn't talk with a Cornish accent. She was pleased to see them and gave them a warm welcome. She took them upstairs to a bathroom, big but primitive. There was one tap only and that was for cold water. It ran very slowly indeed!

But it was really cold, and was lovely and soft to wash in. The tired children cleaned themselves and combed their hair.

They had two bedrooms between them, one for the girls and one for the boys. They were rather small, with little windows that gave a meagre amount of light, so that the rooms looked dark even in the bright evening sunshine.

They were bare little rooms, with two beds in each, one chair, one chest of drawers, one cupboard and two small rugs. Nothing else! But, oh! the views out of the windows!

Miles and miles of countryside, set with cornfields, pasture land, tall hedges and glimpses of winding lanes; heather was out on some of the hills, blazing purple in the sun; and, gleaming in the distance was the dark blue brilliance of the Cornish sea. Lovely!

'We'll bike to the sea as soon as we can,' said Dick, trying to flatten the few hairs that would stick up straight on the top of his head. 'There are caves on this coast. We'll explore them. I wonder if Mrs Penruthlan would give us picnic lunches so that we can go off for the day when we want to.'

'Sure to,' said Julian. 'She's a pet. I've never

felt so welcome in my life. Are we ready? Come on down, then. I'm beginning to feel very empty indeed.'

The tea that awaited them was truly magnificent. A huge ham gleaming as pink as Timmy's tongue; a salad fit for a king. In fact, as Dick said, fit for *several* kings, it was so enormous. It had in it everything that anyone could possibly want.

'Lettuce, tomatoes, onions, radishes, mustard and cress, carrot grated up – this *is* carrot, isn't it, Mrs Penruthlan?' said Dick. 'And lots of hard-boiled eggs.'

There was an enormous tureen of new potatoes, all gleaming with melted butter, scattered with parsley. There was a big bottle of home-made salad cream.

'Look at that cream cheese, too,' gasped Dick, quite overcome. 'And that fruitcake. And are those drop-scones, or what? Are we supposed to have something of everything, Mrs Penruthlan?'

'Oh, yes,' she said, smiling at Dick's pleasure. 'And there's a cherry tart made with our own cherries, and our own cream with it. I know what hungry children are. I've had seven of my own, all married and gone away. So I have to make do with other people's when I can get them.'

'I'm really glad you happened to get hold of *us*,' said Dick, beginning on ham and salad. 'Well, we'll keep you busy, Mrs Penruthlan. We've all got big appetites!'

'Ah, I've not met any children yet that could eat like mine,' said Mrs Penruthlan, sounding really sorry. 'Same as I've not met any man that can eat like Mr Penruthlan. He's a good eater, he is. He'll be in soon.'

'I hope we'll leave enough for him,' said Anne, looking at the ham and the half-empty salad dish. 'No wonder my uncle's friend, the man who came to stay here, went away as fat as butter, Mrs Penruthlan.'

'Oh, the poor man!' said their hostess, who was now filling up their glasses with rich, creamy milk. 'Thin as my husband's old rake, he was, and all his bones showing and creaking. He said "No" to this and "No" to that, but I took no notice of him at all. If he didn't eat his lunch, I'd take his tray away and tidy it up, and then in ten minutes I'd take it back again and say: "Lunch-time, sir, and I hope you're hungry!" And he'd start all over again, and maybe that time he'd really tuck in!'

'But didn't he know you'd already taken him his lunch-tray once?' said Julian, astonished. 'He *must* have been a dreamer.'

'I took his tray in three times once,' said Mrs Penruthlan. 'So you be careful in case I do the same kind of thing to you!'

'I'd love it!' grinned Julian. 'Yes, please, I'd like some more ham. *And* more salad.'

Footsteps came outside the room, on the stone floor of the hall. The door opened and the farmer himself came in. The children stared at him in awe.

He was a strange and magnificent figure of a man – tall, well over six feet, broadly built, and extremely dark. His mane of hair was black and curly, and his eyes were as black as his hair.

'This is Mr Penruthlan,' said his wife, and the children stood up to shake hands, feeling half afraid of this dark giant.

He nodded his head and shook hands. His hand was enormous, and was covered with hairs so thick and black that it was like fur. Anne thought that it would be nice and soft to stroke, like a cat's back!

He didn't say a word, but sat down and let his wife serve him.

'Well, Mr Penruthlan,' she said, 'and how's the cow getting along?'

'Ah,' said the farmer, taking a plate of ham. The children gazed at the slices in awe, seven or eight of them!

'Oh, I'm glad she's all right,' said Mrs Penruthlan, stacking up some dirty plates. 'And is the calf a sweet little thing – and what's the colour?'

'Ah,' said Mr Penruthlan, nodding his head.

'Red and white, like its mum! That's good, isn't it?' said his wife, who seemed to have a miraculous way of interpreting his 'Ahs'. 'What shall we call it?'

Everybody badly wanted to say 'Ah', but nobody dared. However, Mr Penruthlan didn't say 'Ah' that time, but something that sounded like 'Ock'.

'Yes, we'll call it Buttercup, then,' said his wife, nodding her head. 'You always have such good ideas, Mr Penruthlan.'

It sounded odd to hear her call her husband by

his surname like that, and yet, somehow, the children couldn't imagine this giant of a man even owning a name like Jack or Jim. They went on with their own meal, enjoying every minute of it, watching Mr Penruthlan shovel in great mouthfuls, and working his way quickly through every dish. Mrs Penruthlan saw them watching him.

'He's a good eater, isn't he?' she said, proudly. 'So were all my children. When they were at home, I was kept really busy, but now, with only Mr Penruthlan to feed, I feel completely lost. That's why I like people here. You'll tell me if you don't have enough to eat, won't you?'

They all laughed, and Timmy barked. He'd had a wonderful meal, too; it was the remains of Mrs Penruthlan's big stockpot, and was very tasty indeed. He had also got the largest bone he'd ever had in his life. The only thing that really worried the well-fed Timmy now was, where could he put the bone out of the way of the farm dogs?

Mr Penruthlan suddenly made a strange noise and began undoing a trouser pocket at the back.

'Oo-ah!' he said, and brought out a dirty, folded piece of paper.

He handed it to his wife, who unfolded it and

read it. She looked up at the children, smiling.

'Now, *here's* a bit of excitement!' she said. 'The Barnies will be along this week! You'll love them.'

'What *are* the Barnies?' asked George, puzzled at Mrs Penruthlan's evident pleasure and excitement.

'Oh, they're travelling actors that wander around the countryside and perform in our big barns,' said Mrs Penruthlan. 'There are no cinemas for miles, you know, so the Barnies are always very welcome.'

'Oh, you call them Barnies because they use your barns for their shows,' said Anne, seeing the light. 'Yes, we'd love to see them, Mrs Penruthlan. Will they perform in *your* barn?'

'Yes. We'll have all the village here when the Barnies come,' said Mrs Penruthlan, her cheeks going red with delight. 'And maybe people from Trelin Village, too. Now, there's a treat for you!'

'Ah,' said Mr Penruthlan, and nodded his great head.

Evidently he liked the Barnies, too. He gave a sudden laugh and said something short and completely incomprehensible.

'He says you'll like Clopper the horse,' said his wife, laughing. 'The things he does! The way he sits down and crosses his legs. Well, you wait and see. That horse!'

This sounded astonishing. A horse that sat down and crossed its legs? Julian winked at Dick. They would certainly see the Barnies!

3 The first evening

After their wonderful tea the four children didn't really feel like doing very much. Dick thought he ought to mend his puncture, but wasn't sure that he could bend over properly!

Mrs Penruthlan began to stack the dishes and clear away. George and Anne offered to help her.

'Well, that's kind of you, Anne and Georgina,' said the farmer's wife. 'But you're tired tonight. You can give me a hand some other time. By the way, which of you is which?'

'I'm Anne,' said Anne.

'And I'm George, not Georgina,' said George. 'So please don't call me that. I hate it. I always wanted to be a boy, so I only like to be called George.'

'What she really means is that she won't answer unless you *do* call her George,' said Anne. 'Well, if you really are sure you don't need our help, we'll go out with the boys.'

So out they went, George really looking far more like a boy than a girl, with her jeans and shirt and her short, curly hair and freckled face. She put her hands in her pockets and tried to walk like Dick!

Dick soon found his puncture and mended it. Mr Penruthlan came by with some straw for his cow and new calf. The boys watched him in awe, for he was carrying almost a wagonload of straw tied up in bales! What strength he had! He nodded to them and passed without a word.

'Why doesn't he talk?' wondered Dick. 'Maybe all his seven children take after their talkative mum, and he never had a chance to get a word in. And it's too late now, he's forgotten how to!'

They laughed.

'What a giant of a man,' said Julian. 'I hope I grow as big as that.'

'I don't, I'd hate to have my bare feet poking out of the bottom of the bed every night,' said Dick. 'There. I've finished that puncture. See the nail that made it? I must have run over it on the way to the station this morning.'

'Look at Timmy,' said Julian. 'He's having the

time of his life with those farm dogs, acting just like a puppy!'

So he was, bounding here and there, rushing around the dogs and then rushing away, jumping on first one and then another, till they all went down in an excited, yapping scrum, the little Scottie doing his best to keep up with everything!

'Timmy's going to have a good time here,' said Dick. 'And he'll soon lose his beautiful waistline if he eats as well as we do!'

'We'll take him on long bike rides,' said Julian. 'He can't grow much tummy if he runs for miles!'

The girls came up just then. A few feet behind trotted a little boy, bare-footed, shock-headed and very dirty.

'Who's this?' said Dick.

'I don't know,' said George. 'He suddenly appeared behind us and has been following us ever since.'

The boy wore a ragged pair of jeans and an old jumper. He was black-eyed and burnt dark brown by the sun. He stood a few feet away and stared.

'Who are you?' said Dick.

The boy went back a few steps in fright. He shook his head.

'I said, who are you?' said Dick again. 'What's your name?'

'Yan,' said the boy.

'All right, Yan. You can go home now,' said Anne.

'I want to stay,' said the boy solemnly.

And stay he did, following them about everywhere, gazing at all they did with the utmost curiosity, as if he'd never in his life seen children before!

'He's like a mosquito,' said Dick. 'Always buzzing around. Hey, Yan!'

'Yes?'

'You'd better go. Go home!' said Dick sternly. Yan stared.

Mrs Penruthlan came out and heard all this.

'Yan bothering you?' she said. 'He's as full of curiosity as a cat. Go home, Yan. Take this to your grandad. And here's some for you.'

Yan came up eagerly and took the packet of food Mrs Penruthlan held out to him, and the slice of cake. He ran off without a word, his bare feet making no sound.

'Who is he?' asked George.

'He's a poor little thing,' said the farmer's wife. 'He's got no family except for his great-grandad, and there's more than eighty years between them! The old man is our shepherd. Do you see that hill over there, well, he's got a hut on the other side, and there he lives, winter and summer alike, and that child with him.'

'Doesn't he to go to school?' asked Julian.

'No,' said Mrs Penruthlan. 'He plays truant nearly all the time. You ought to go and talk to his great-grandad. His dad was one of the Wreckers on this coast, and he can tell you some strange stories about those dreadful days.'

'We'll definitely go and talk to him,' said Dick. 'I'd forgotten that this Cornish coast was the home of Wreckers. They shone false lights to bring ships in close to shore, so that they'd be smashed to pieces on the rocks, didn't they?'

'Yes, and then they robbed the poor, groaning ship when she was helpless,' said Mrs Penruthlan. 'And it's said they paid no heed to the drowning people, either. Those were wicked days.'

'How far is it to cycle to the sea?' said George. 'I can see it from my bedroom window.'

'Oh, it won't take you more than ten minutes,' said the farmer's wife. 'Go tomorrow, if you like. You all look very tired now. Why don't you take a short walk and go to bed? I'll have a snack ready for you when you come in.'

'Oh, we couldn't *possibly* eat any more tonight, thank you,' said Dick, hurriedly. 'But the walk's a good idea. We'd like to see around the farm.'

Mrs Penruthlan left them, and Dick looked around at the others.

'A snack!' he said. 'I never thought I'd groan at the thought. But I bet Mr Penruthlan will want a really good snack when he comes in. Come on, let's go up by those sheds.'

They went off together, Timmy following behind with his four friends, their tails wagging amiably. It was still a lovely evening, and a cool breeze came down from the hills, making it lovelier still. The children wandered around, enjoying the familiar farm sights, the ducks on the pond, a few hens still clucking around, the grey sheep dotting the hills. Cows were peacefully grazing and an old farm horse came to a gate to stare at them.

They rubbed his velvety nose, and he bent down

to sniff at Timmy, whom he didn't know. Timmy sniffed solemnly back.

They went into the barns and looked around, big, dark, sweet-smelling places, stored with many things. Dick was sure that the biggest one would be the one used by the Barnies.

'I bet they'll be good fun,' he said. 'It must be wonderful to wander around the countryside with all your belongings done up in a parcel or two, and then amaze the country people with your songs and dances and acting. I wouldn't mind trying it myself! I'm pretty good at magic tricks, for instance!'

'Yes, you are,' said Anne. 'Wouldn't it be fun if we could give a little show too, if the Barnies would let us join them just for one evening?'

'We wouldn't be allowed to because we're "foreigners",' said Dick grinning. 'Hey, what's that, over there, behind that sack?'

Timmy at once went over to see, and stood there barking. The others went over to look.

'It's Yan again,' said Julian. He pulled the boy out from his hiding place. 'What are you following us around for?' he asked. 'Go and find your grandad before you eat all the food Mrs

Penruthlan gave you. Go on now.'

He watched the boy go out of the barn, and into the next field.

'Let's go and see that grandad of his one day and see if he really *has* got anything interesting to say about the old Wreckers.'

'Let's go back now,' said Dick, yawning. 'I've seen enough of this place to know I'm going to like it a lot. I'm going to like my bed tonight too. Coming, Ju?'

They all felt the same as Dick. His yawn had set them yawning too, and they thought longingly of bed. They made their way back to the farm, followed closely by Timmy at their heels, and the other four dogs a respectful distance away.

They said goodnight to the two Penruthlans, who were sitting peacefully listening to their radio. Mrs Penruthlan wanted to come up with them but they wouldn't let her.

They said goodnight to the farmer, who grunted 'Ah!' without even looking at them, and went on listening to the radio programme. Then up the stairs they went, and into their rooms.

When Julian was in bed and almost asleep he heard a scrabbling noise outside his window. He half opened his eyes, and listened. He hoped it wasn't rats! If it was, Anne would probably hear them too, and be scared, and Timmy would hear them and bark the place down!

The scrabbling noise came again. Julian spoke softly to Dick. 'Dick! Are you awake? Did you hear that noise at the window?'

No answer. Dick was sound asleep, dreaming that he had a puncture in his foot and couldn't walk till it was mended! Julian lay and listened. Yes, there it was again, and now surely there was someone trying to peer in at the tiny window?

He slid out of bed and went to the side of the window.

Thick ivy grew outside. Somebody was still there, as Julian could see the leaves shaking.

He put his head suddenly out of the window, and a scared face, very close to his, stared in fright.

'Yan! What do you think you're doing?' said Julian. 'I'll lose my temper with you if you go on like this, staring and peering! What's so strange about us?'

Yan was terrified. He suddenly slithered down the ivy like a cat, landed with a slight thud on the ground and then ran off into the twilight at top speed.

'I hope he's not going to follow us around all the time,' thought Julian, getting into bed again. 'Bother him! Now he's made me wide awake!'

But it wasn't long before Julian was sleeping as soundly as Dick. Neither of them stirred until a cockerel outside their window decided that it was time the whole world woke up, and crowed at the top of his voice.

'Cock-a-doodle-DOO!'

The boys woke with a jump. The early sun streamed into the room, and Julian glanced at his watch. How early it was! And yet he could hear movements downstairs that told him Mrs Penruthlan was up and about, and so was her giant of a husband.

He fell asleep again, and was awakened by a loud knock at his door, and Mrs Penruthlan's voice. 'It's half past seven, and breakfast will be on the table for you at eight. Wake up!'

How lovely to wake in a strange place at the beginning of a holiday, to think of swimming and biking and picnicking and eating and drinking, forgetting all about exams and rules! The four children and Timmy stretched themselves and stared at the sunshine outside. What a day!

Downstairs breakfast awaited them.

'Wonderful!' said Dick, eyeing the bacon and fried eggs, the cold ham, and the home-made jam and marmalade. 'Mrs Penruthlan, your seven children must have been very sorry to leave home. I think, if I'd been one of them, I'd have stayed with you for the rest of my life!'

4 Down in the cove

The first three days at Tremannon Farm were lazy uneventful days, full of sunshine, good food, dogs – and Yan.

He really was a nuisance. The four children seemed to have a real fascination for him, and he trailed them everywhere, following them barefooted. He turned up behind hedges, along lanes, at their picnicking places, his dark eyes watching them intently.

'What's the use of telling him to go?' groaned Julian. 'He disappears behind one hedge and appears out of another. You'd think he'd get bored, doing this shadowing business all the time. What's the point of it, anyway?'

'No point,' said George. 'Just curiosity. What I can't understand is why Timmy puts up with him. You'd think he'd bark or growl or something, but he's completely silly with Yan, lets him play with him, and roll him over as if he was a mad puppy.'

'Well, I'm going to find this great-grandad of his tomorrow, and tell him to keep Yan with him,' said Julian. 'He's so annoying. I want to swat him like a gnat, always buzzing around us. Oh, there he is again!'

So he was. A pair of dark eyes were gazing around a tree trunk, half hidden by a sheaf of leaves. Timmy bounded up to him in glee, and made such a fuss of Yan that George was completely disgusted.

'Timmy! Come here!' she called, imperiously. 'Don't you understand that you ought not to encourage Yan? I'm ashamed of you!'

Timmy put his tail down and went to her. He sat down beside her with a bump. Dick laughed.

'He's sulking! He won't look at you, George! He's turning his head away on purpose!'

Yan ran away as fast as a hare, and seemed suddenly to disappear into thin air. He had an amazing way of vanishing, and an equally remarkable way of appearing again.

'I don't like that kid,' said Julian. 'He makes me shiver down my back whenever I see him suddenly peering somewhere.'

'He can't be a bad kid, though, because Timmy

likes him so much,' said Anne, who had great faith in Timmy's judgement. 'Timmy never likes anyone horrible.'

'Well, he's made a mistake this time, then,' said George, who was cross with Timmy. 'He's being very stupid. I'm not pleased with you, Timmy!'

'Let's go down to the sea and swim,' said Dick. 'We'll go on our bikes and Yan won't be able to pop up and watch us there.'

They took their bikes and rode off to the coast. Mrs Penruthlan made them sandwiches and gave them fruitcake and drinks to take with them. They saw Yan watching them from behind a hedge as they went.

They took the road to the sea. It was no more than a narrow lane, and wound around like a stream, twisting and turning so that they couldn't get up any speed at all.

'Look – the sea!' cried Dick as they rounded one last bend.

The lane had run down between two high, rocky cliffs, and in front of them was a cove into which raced enormous breakers, throwing spray high into the air.

They left their bikes at the top of the cove, and

went behind some big rocks to change into swimming things. When they came out, Julian looked at the sea. It was calm beyond the rocks, but over these the waters raged fiercely and it was impossible to venture in.

They walked a little way around the cliffs, and came to a great pool lying in a rock hollow.

'Just the thing!' cried George and plunged in. 'Oh, it's cold!'

It should have been hot from the sun, but every now and again an extra large wave broke right into the pool itself, bringing in cooler water. It was fun when that happened. The four of them swam to their hearts' content, and Timmy had a lovely time too.

They picnicked on the rocks, with spray flying around them, and then went to explore around the foot of the cliffs.

'This is exciting,' said George. 'Caves, and more caves, and yet more caves! And cove after cove, all as lovely as the one before. I suppose when the tide's in, all these coves are shoulder-high in water.'

'Yes,' said Julian, who was keeping a very sharp eye indeed on the tide. 'And lots of these caves

would be flooded too. No wonder Mrs Penruthlan
warned us so seriously about the tides here! I
wouldn't want to try and climb up these cliffs if
we were caught!'

Anne looked up and shivered. They were very
steep and high. They frowned down at her as if to
say 'We stand no nonsense from anyone! So look
after yourself!'

'I don't believe it! Look there, isn't that Yan?'
said Dick, suddenly.

He pointed to a rock covered with seaweed.
Peering from behind it was Yan!

'He must have run all the way here, and found
us,' said Julian. 'Well, we'll leave him here. It's
time we went. The tide's coming in. It'll serve him
right to find us gone as soon as he arrives. He
must be mad!'

'Do you think he knows about the tide?' said
Anne, looking worried. 'I mean, knows that it's
coming in and might catch him?'

'Of course he knows!' said Julian. 'Don't be
silly. But we'll wait and have our tea at the top
part of the cove, if you like. That's the only way
back, if he wants to escape the tide, short of
climbing the cliff, which no one would be mad

enough to try!'

They had put aside some cake and biscuits for their tea, and they found a good picnicking place at the top of the cove where they had left their bikes. They settled down to munch the solid fruitcake that Mrs Penruthlan had given them. There was no doubt about it, she was a wonderful cook!

The tide swept in at a great rate, and soon the noise of enormous waves pounding on the rocks grew louder.

'Yan hasn't appeared yet,' said Anne. 'Do you think he's all right?'

'He must be having a good wetting if he's still there,' said Dick. 'I think we'd better go and see. He's annoying but I don't want him to be drowned.'

The two boys went down the cove as far as they could, peering around the cliff to where they had seen Yan hiding. But how different it all looked now!

'The beach is gone already!' said Julian, startled. 'I can see how easily anyone could get caught by the tide now. See that last wave, it swept right into that cave we explored!'

'What's happened to Yan?' said Dick. 'He's nowhere to be seen. He didn't come out of the cove; we've been sitting there all the time. Where is he?'

Dick sounded worried, and Julian began to feel scared too. He hesitated. Should they wade over the rocks a little way? The next wave decided him. It would be madness to do any such thing! Another wave like that and both he and Dick would be flung off the rock they were standing on!

'Look out, here comes an even bigger one!' yelled Julian, and the two boys leapt off their rock and raced back up the cove. Even so, the wave lapped right up to their feet.

They went back to the girls.

'Can't see him anywhere,' said Julian, speaking more cheerfully than he felt. 'The whole beach is covered with the tide now, more than covered. The lower caves are full too.'

'He – he won't be drowned, will he?' said Anne, fearfully.

'Oh, I expect he can look after himself,' said Julian. 'He's used to this coast. Come on, it's time we went.'

They all rode off, Timmy running beside their

bikes. Nobody said anything. They couldn't help feeling worried about Yan. What could have happened to him?

They arrived at the farm and put their bikes away. They went in to find Mrs Penruthlan. They told her about Yan, and how he'd disappeared.

'You don't think he might have been swept off his feet and drowned, do you?' asked Anne.

Mrs Penruthlan laughed. 'Good heavens, no! That boy knows his way around the countryside and the seashore blindfold. He's cleverer than you think. He never misses anything! He's a poor little thing, but he looks after himself all right!'

This was comforting. Perhaps Yan would turn up again, with his dark eyes fixed unblinking on them!

After a tea as good as any they had ever had, they went for a walk down the honeysuckle-scented lanes, accompanied as usual by the five dogs. They sat on a stile, and Dick handed around some barley sugar.

'Look!' said George suddenly. 'Do you see what I see? Look!'

She nodded her head towards an oak tree in the hedge, not far off. The others stared up into it.

Two dark eyes stared back. Yan! He'd followed them as usual, and had hidden himself to watch them. Anne was so tremendously relieved to see him that she called to him in delight.

'Oh, Yan! Have a barley sugar?'

Yan slithered down the tree at top speed and came up. He held out his hand for the barley sugar. For the first time he smiled, and his dirty, sulky face lit up. Anne stared at him. He was all right after all! His eyes shone and twinkled, and a dimple came in each cheek.

'Here you are, have a couple more sweets,' Dick said, very glad to see that the small boy hadn't been drowned.

Yan almost snatched them from him! It was obvious that he very, very seldom had any sweets! Timmy was making a fuss of him as usual. He lay down on his back and rolled over Yan's feet. He licked his fingers, and jumped up at him, almost knocking the boy down. Yan laughed and fell on Timmy, rolling over and over with him. Julian, Dick and Anne watched and laughed.

But George wasn't pleased. Timmy was her dog, and she didn't like him to make a fuss of anyone she disapproved of. She was glad that Yan was safe but she still didn't like him! So she scowled, and Julian nudged Dick to make him see the scowl. George saw him and scowled worse than ever.

'You'll be sorry you gave him sweets,' she said. 'He'll hang around us worse than ever now.'

Yan came up after a minute or two, sucking all three sweets at once, so that his right cheek was very swollen indeed.

'Come and see my grandad,' he said. 'I've told him about you all. He'll tell you lots of things.'

He stared at them all seriously.

'Grandad likes sweets too,' he added, solemnly.

Julian laughed. 'All right. We'll come and see him tomorrow afternoon. Now you go home. Understand?'

'Yes,' said Yan, nodding his head. He took the three sweets out of his mouth, looked at them to see how much he'd sucked them, and then put them back again.

'I've just thought,' said Julian, 'how did you get away from that beach this afternoon? Did you climb that cliff?'

'No,' said Yan, shifting his sweets to the other cheek. 'I came the Wreckers' Way. My grandad showed me.'

He was off and away before anyone could ask him another question. The four looked at one another.

'Did you hear that?' said Julian. 'He went the Wreckers' Way. What's that, do you think? We must have been on one of the beaches the Wreckers used long, long ago.'

'Yes. But how did he get off that beach, and away to safety?' said Dick. 'I'd like to know more about the Wreckers' Way! Let's definitely pay a visit to Great-Grandad tomorrow. He might have some very interesting things to tell us.'

'Fine, we'll go and see him,' said George, getting up. 'But just you remember what I said. Yan will pester us more than ever now we've encouraged him.'

'Oh well, he doesn't seem such a bad kid after all,' said Dick. 'And if he persuades Grandad to let us into the secret of Wreckers' Way, we might have some fun doing a bit of exploring. Don't you think so, Ju?'

'It might even lead to an adventure,' said Julian, laughing at Anne's serious face. 'Cheer up, Anne. I can't even *smell* an adventure in Tremannon.

I'm just pulling your leg!'

'I think you're wrong,' said Anne. 'If *you* can't smell one somewhere, I can. I don't want to, but I can!'

5 Yan – and his grandad

The next day was Sunday. It made no difference to the time that the two Penruthlans got up, however. As Mrs Penruthlan said, the cows and horses, hens and ducks didn't approve of late Sunday breakfasts! They wanted attending to at exactly the same time each day!

'Will you be going to church?' asked Mrs Penruthlan. 'It's a beautiful walk across the fields to Tremannon Church, and you'd like Parson. He's a good man, he is.'

'Yes, we're all going,' said Julian. 'We can tie Timmy up outside. He's used to that. And we thought we'd go up and see your old shepherd this afternoon, Mrs Penruthlan, and see what tales he has to tell.'

'Yan'll show you the way,' said the farmer's wife, bustling off to her cooking. 'I'll get you a lovely Sunday lunch. Do you like fresh fruit salad with cream?'

'Yes!' said everyone at once.

'Can we help you to do something?' said Anne. 'I've just seen all the peas you're going to shell. Piles of them! And don't you want help with those redcurrants? I love getting the currants off their stalks with a fork!'

'Well, you'll have a few minutes before you go to church, I expect,' said Mrs Penruthlan, looking pleased. 'It *would* be a bit of help today.

Soon the noise of the popping of pods was to be heard, a very pleasant noise, Anne thought. The four of them sat on the big kitchen step, out in the sun, with Timmy sitting beside them, watching with interest. He didn't stay with them long though.

Up came his four friends, the little Scottie trotting valiantly behind, trying to keep up with the longer legs of the others.

'Woof!' said the biggest collie. Timmy wagged his tail politely, but didn't stir.

'Woof!' said the collie again, and pranced around invitingly.

'Timmy! He says "Will you come and play?"' said George. 'Aren't you going? You're no help with shelling peas, and you keep breathing down my neck.'

Timmy gave George a flying lick and leapt off the step joyfully. He pounced on the Scottie, rolled him over, and then took on all three collies at once. They were big, strong dogs, but no match for Timmy!

'Look at him,' said George, proudly. 'He can manage the whole lot single-handed.'

'Single-footed!' said Dick. 'He's faster than even that biggest collie and stronger than the whole lot. Good old Tim. He's come in really useful in some of our adventures!'

'I'm sure he will again,' said Julian. 'I'd rather have one Timmy than two police dogs.'

'I expect his ears are burning, the way we're talking about him!' said Anne. 'Oh, sorry, Dick, that pod popped unexpectedly!'

'That's the second lot of peas you've shot all over me,' said Dick, scrabbling inside his shirt. 'I *must* just find one that went down my neck, or I'll be fidgeting all through church.'

'You always do,' said Anne. 'Look – isn't that Yan?'

It was! He came sidling up and gave them a quick smile that once more entirely changed his sulky little face. He held out his hand, palm upwards.

'What does he want?' said Dick. 'Oh, he's asking for a sweet.'

'Don't give him one,' said Julian, quickly. 'Yan, if you want a sweet, you can help pod these peas.'

Mrs Penruthlan appeared at once.

'But see he washes those filthy hands first,' she commanded, and disappeared again.

Yan looked at his hands, then put them under his armpits.

'Go and wash them,' said Julian. But Yan shook his head, and sat down a little way away from them.

'All right. Don't wash your hands. Don't shell the peas. Don't have a sweet,' said George.

Yan scowled at George. He didn't seem to like her any more than she liked him. He waited till someone split a pod, and a few peas shot out on the ground instead of into the dish. Then he darted at them, picked them up and ate them. He was as quick as a cat.

'My grandad says come and see him,' announced Yan. 'I'll take you.'

'Right,' said Julian. 'We'll come this afternoon. We'll get Mrs Penruthlan to pack us up a basket, and we'll have tea in the hills. You can share it if you wash your hands and face.'

'Oh, here's Timmy come back,' said George. 'I *will* not have him fawn around that boy. Here, Timmy!'

But Timmy darted to Yan with the greatest delight and pawed at him to come and have a game. They began to roll over and over like two puppies.

'If you're going to church, you'd better get ready,' said Mrs Penruthlan, appearing again, this time with arms floured up to the elbow. 'Oh, what a lot of peas you've done for me!'

'I wish I had time to do the redcurrants,' said Anne. 'We've almost finished the peas, anyway, Mrs Penruthlan. We've done thousands, I should think!'

'Ah, Mr Penruthlan is very fond of peas,' said the farmer's wife. 'He can eat a whole bowlful at one sitting.'

She disappeared again. The children went to get ready for church, and then off they went. It was a lovely walk over the fields, with honeysuckle trailing everywhere!

The church was small and old and lovely. Yan went with them, trailing behind, right to the church door. When he saw George tying Timmy up to a railing, he sat down beside him and looked pleased. George didn't look pleased, however. Now Timmy and Yan would play about together all the time she was in church! How annoying!

The church was cool and dark, except for three lovely stained-glass windows through which the sun poured, its brilliance dimmed by the colours of the glass. 'Parson' was as nice as Mrs Penruthlan had said, a friendly person whose words were listened to by everyone, from an old woman bent almost double in a corner to a solemn-eyed five-year-old clutching her mother's hand.

It was dazzling to come out into the sun again from the cool dimness of the church. Timmy barked a welcome. Yan was still there, sitting with his arm around Timmy's neck. He gave them his sudden smile, and untied Timmy, who promptly went mad and tore out of the churchyard at sixty miles an hour. He always did that when he'd been tied up.

'Come and see Grandad,' said Yan to Dick,

and pulled at his arm.

'This afternoon,' said Dick. 'You can show us the way. Come after lunch.'

So, after the children had had a lunch of beef and carrots, with a dumpling each, and lots of peas and new potatoes, followed by a delicious fruit salad and cream, Yan appeared at the door to take them to see his grandad.

'Did you see the amount of peas that Mr Penruthlan got through?' said Anne, in awe. 'I think he really *did* manage a bowlful all to himself. I wish he'd say something besides "Ah" and "Ock" and the other strange sounds he makes. Conversation is very difficult with him.'

'Is Yan taking you up to Grandad?' called Mrs Penruthlan. 'I'll put a few cakes in the basket for him, too, then, and for Grandad.'

'*Don't* give us too much,' begged Dick. 'We only want a snack, just to keep us going till tea.'

But all the same the basket was very heavy when Mrs Penruthlan had finished packing it!

It was a long walk over the fields to the shepherd's hut. Yan led the way proudly. They crossed the fields and climbed stiles, walked up narrow cart-paths, and at last came to a cone-shaped hill on which sheep grazed peacefully. Half-grown lambs, wearing their woolly coats, unlike the shorn sheep, gambolled here and there – then remembered that they were nearly grown up, and walked sedately.

The old shepherd was sitting outside his hut, smoking a clay pipe. He wasn't very big, and he seemed shrivelled up, like an apple stored too long. But there was still sweetness in him, and the children liked him at once. He had Yan's sudden smile, that lit up eyes that were still as blue as the summer sky above.

His face had a thousand wrinkles that creased and ran into one another when he smiled. His shaggy eyebrows, curly beard and hair were all grey, as grey as the woolly coats of the sheep he'd lived with all his life.

'You're welcome,' he said, in his slow Cornish voice. 'Yan told me about you.'

'We've brought our tea to share with you,' said Dick. 'We'll have it later on. Is it true that your dad was one of the Wreckers in the old days?'

The old man nodded his head. Julian got out a bag of boiled sweets, and offered them to the old man. He took one eagerly. Yan edged up at once and was given one too.

Judging by the crunching that went on Grandad still had plenty of teeth! When the sweet had gone, he began to talk. He talked slowly and simply, and sometimes paused to find a word he wanted.

'Living with sheep all his life doesn't make for easy talking,' thought Julian, interested in this old man with the wise, keen eyes. He must be much more at home with sheep than with human beings.

Grandad certainly had some interesting things to tell them, dreadful things, Anne thought.

'You've seen the rocks down on Tremannon coast,' began Grandad. 'Wicked rocks they are, hungry for ships and men. Many a ship's been wrecked on purpose! Aye, you can look disbelieving-like, but it's true.'

'How did they get wrecked on purpose?' asked Dick. 'Were they lured here by a false light, or something?'

The old man lowered his voice as if he was afraid of being overheard.

'Way back up the coast, more than a hundred years ago, there was a light set to guide the ships that sail around here,' said Grandad. 'They were to sail towards that light, and then hug the coast and avoid the rocks that stood out to sea. They were safe then. But, on wild nights, a light was set two miles farther down the coast, to confuse lost ships, and drag them to the rocks around Tremannon coves.'

'That's horrible!' said Anne and George together. 'How *could* people do that?'

'It's amazing what people will do,' said Grandad, nodding his head. 'Take my old dad now – a kind man he was and went to church, and took me with him. But he was the one that set the false light burning every time, and sent men to watch the ship coming in on the rocks – crashing over them and breaking into pieces.'

'Did you – did you ever see a ship crashing to its death?' asked Dick, imagining the groaning of the sailing ships, and the groaning of the men flung into the raging sea.

'Aye, I did,' said Grandad, his eyes taking on a very far-away look. 'I was sent to the cove with the men, and had to hold a lantern to confuse the ship again when she came to the rocks. Poor thing, she groaned like a live thing when she ran into those wicked rocks, and split into pieces. And the next day I went to the cove to help get the goods that were scattered all around the cove. There were lots drowned that night, and—'

'Don't tell us about that,' said Dick, feeling sick. 'Where did they flash the false light from? From these hills, or from the cliff somewhere?'

'I'll show you where my dad flashed it from,' said Grandad, and he got up slowly. 'There's only one place on these hills where you could see the light flashing. The Wreckers had to find somewhere well hidden, so that their light couldn't be seen from inland, or the police would stop it, but it could be seen clearly by any ship on the sea near this coast!'

He took them around his hill, and then pointed towards the coast. Set between two hills there the roof of a house could just be seen, and from it rose a tower. It could only be seen from that one spot! Dick took a few steps to each side of it, and at once the house disappeared behind one or other of the hills on each side of it.

'I was the only one who ever knew the false light could be seen from inland,' said Grandad, pointing with his pipe-stem towards the far-off square tower. 'I was watching lambs one night up here, and I saw the light flashing. 'And I heard there was a ship wrecked down in Tremannon cove that night so I reckoned it was the Wreckers at work.'

'Did you often see the light flashing over there, when you watched the sheep?' asked George.

'Oh yes, many a time,' said the shepherd. 'And always on wild, stormy nights, when ships were labouring along, and in trouble, looking for some light to guide them into shore. Then a light would flare out over there, and I'd say to myself "God help those sailors tonight, for it's sure that nobody else will!"'

'How horrible!' said George, appalled at such wickedness. 'You must be glad that you never see that false light shining there on stormy nights now!'

Grandad looked at George, and his eyes were scared and strange. He lowered his voice and spoke to George as if she were a boy.

'Young man,' he said, 'that light still flares on dark and stormy nights. The place is a ruin, and jackdaws build in the tower. But three times this year I've seen that light again! Come a stormy night it'll flare again! I know it in my bones, I know it in my bones!'

6 A strange tale

The four children shivered suddenly in the hot sun, as they listened to the shepherd's strange words. Were they true? Did the Wreckers' light still flash in the old tower on wild and stormy nights? But why should it? Surely no Wreckers any longer did their dreadful work on this lonely rocky coast?

Dick voiced the thoughts of the others. 'But surely there are no wrecks on this coast now? Isn't there a good lighthouse farther up, to warn ships to keep right out to sea?'

Grandad nodded his grey head. 'Yes. There's a lighthouse, and there's not been a wreck along this coast for more years than I can remember. But I tell you that light flares up just as it used to do. I see it with my own eyes, and there's nothing wrong with them yet!'

'I've seen it too,' put in Yan, suddenly.

Grandad looked at Yan, annoyed.

'You hold your tongue,' he commanded. 'You've never seen the light. You sleep like a babe at night.'

'I've seen it,' said Yan, obstinately.

Dick changed the subject. 'Grandad, do you know anything about the Wreckers' Way?' he asked. 'Is it a secret way to get down to the coves from inland? Was it used by the Wreckers?'

Grandad frowned. 'That's a secret,' he said shortly. 'My dad showed it to me, and I swore I'd never tell. We all had to swear and promise that.'

'But Yan said that you taught the way to him,' said Dick, puzzled.

Yan promptly removed himself from the company and disappeared around a clump of bushes. His great-grandad glared around at the disappearing boy.

'Yan! That boy! He doesn't know anything about the Wreckers' Way. It's lost and forgotten by every man living. I'm the last one left who knows of it. Yan! He's dreaming! Maybe he's heard tell of an old Wreckers' Way, but that's all.'

'Oh!' said Dick, disappointed.

He'd hoped that Grandad would tell them the

old way, and then they could go and explore it. Perhaps they could go and search for it, anyway! It would be fun to do that.

Julian came back to the question of the light flashing from the old tower by the coast. He was puzzled.

'Who could possibly flash that light?' he said to Grandad. 'You say the place is a ruin. Are you sure it wasn't lightning you saw? You said it came on a wild and stormy night.'

'It wasn't lightning,' said the old man shortly. 'I first saw that light near ninety years ago, and I tell you I saw it again three times this year, same place, same light, same weather! And if you told me it wasn't flashed by mortal hands, I'd believe you.'

There was a silence after this extraordinary statement. Anne looked over towards the far-off tower that showed just between the two distant hills. How strange that this spot where they were standing was the only place from which the tower could be seen from inland. The Wreckers had been clever to choose a spot like that to flash a light from. No one but old Grandad up on the hills could possibly have seen the light and guessed what was going on, no one but the callous Wreckers themselves.

Grandad delved deep into more memories stored in his mind. He poured them out, tales of the old days, strange unbelievable stories. One was about an old woman who was said to be a witch. The things she did!

The four stared at the shepherd, entranced to think they were, in a way, linked with the witches, the Wreckers and the killers of long-ago days, through this old, old man.

Yan appeared again as soon as Julian opened the tea-basket. They had now gone back to the hut, and sat outside in the sunshine, surrounded by nibbling sheep. One or two of the half-grown lambs came up, looking hot in their unshorn woolly coats. They nosed around the shepherd, and he rubbed their woolly noses.

'These are lambs I fed from a bottle,' he explained. 'They always remember. Go away now, Woolly. Cake's wasted on you.'

Yan wolfed half the tea. He gave Anne a quick grin of pure pleasure, showing both his dimples at once. She smiled back. She liked this funny little boy now, and felt sorry for him. She was sure that his Grandad didn't give him enough to eat!

The church bells began to ring, and the sun was now sliding down the sky. 'We must go,' said Julian, reluctantly. 'It's quite a long walk back. Thanks for a very interesting afternoon, Grandad. I expect you'll be glad to be rid of us now, and smoke your pipe in peace with your sheep around you.'

'Aye, I will,' said Grandad, truthfully. 'I'm one for my own company, and I like to think my own thoughts. Long thoughts they are, too, going back nearly a hundred years. If I want to talk, I talk to my sheep. It's wonderful how they listen.'

The children laughed, but Grandad was quite serious, and meant every word he said. They packed up the basket, and said goodbye to the old man.

'What do you think he meant when he talked about the light still flashing in the old tower?' said Dick, as they went over the hills back to the farm. 'What a strange thing to say. Was it true, do you think?'

'There's only one way to find out!' said George, her eyes dancing. 'Wait for a wild and stormy night and go and see!'

'But what about our agreement?' said Julian, solemnly. 'If anything exciting seems about to happen we turn our backs on it. That's what we decided. Don't you remember?'

'Ha!' said George.

'We ought to keep the agreement,' said Anne, doubtfully.

She knew that the others didn't think so!

'Look! Who are all these people?' said Dick, suddenly.

They were just climbing over a stile to cross a lane to another field. They sat on the stile and stared. Some carts were going by, open wagons, their canvas tops folded down. They were the most old-fashioned carts the children had ever seen, not at all like travellers' caravans.

Ten or eleven people were with the wagons, dressed in clothes of other days! Some rode in the wagons and some walked. Some were middle-aged, some were young, but they all looked cheerful and bright.

The children stared. After Grandad's tales of long ago these old-fashioned people seemed just right! For a few moments Anne felt herself back in Grandad's time, when he was a boy. He must have seen people dressed like these!

'Who are they?' she said, wonderingly.

And then the children saw red lettering painted on the biggest cart:

THE BARNIES

'Oh! It's the Barnies! Don't you remember Mrs Penruthlan telling us about them?' said Anne. 'The travelling actors, who perform to the country people around, in the barns. What fun!'

The Barnies waved to the watching children. One man, dressed in velvet and lace, with a sword at his side, and a wig of curly hair, threw a leaflet or two to them. They read them with interest.

THE BARNIES ARE COMING

They will sing, they will dance, they will fiddle.
  They will perform plays of all kinds.
  Edith Wells, the nightingale singer.
  Bonnie Carter, the old-time dancer.
  Janie Coster and her fiddle.
  John Walters, finest tenor in the world.

George Roth – he'll make you laugh!

And Others.

We also present Clopper, the Funniest Horse in the World!

THE BARNIES ARE COMING

'This'll be fun! said George, pleased. She called out to the passing wagons: 'Will you be performing at Tremannon Farm?'

'Oh, yes!' called a man with bright, sparkling eyes. 'We always perform there. You staying there?'

'Yes,' said George. 'We'll look out for you all. Where are you going now?'

'To Poltelly Farm for the night,' called the man. 'We'll be at Tremannon soon.'

The wagons passed, and the cheerful, oddly dressed actors went out of sight.

'Good,' said Dick. 'Their show is sure to be funny. They looked a cheerful lot.'

'All except the man driving the front cart. Did you see him?' said Anne. 'He looked pretty cross, I thought.'

Nobody else had noticed him.

'He was probably in charge of the Barnies,' said Dick. 'And has got all the organisation on his shoulders. Well, come on. Where's Timmy?'

They looked around for him, and George frowned. Yan had followed them as usual, and Timmy was playing with him. Bother Yan! Was he going to trail them all day and every day?

They went back to the peaceful farmhouse. Hens were still clucking around and ducks were quacking. A horse stamped somewhere nearby, and the grunting of pigs came on the air. It all looked perfect.

Footsteps came through the farmyard, and Mr Penruthlan came by. He grunted at them and went into a barn.

Anne spoke in almost a whisper. 'I can imagine him living in the olden days and being a Wrecker. I can really!'

'Yes! I know what you mean,' said Dick. 'He's so fierce-looking and determined. What's the word I want? *Ruthless!* I'm sure he'd have made a good Wrecker!'

'Do you think there *are* any Wreckers now, and that light really *is* flashed to make ships go on the rocks?' said George.

'I wouldn't have thought there were any Wreckers in *this* country, anyway,' said Dick. 'But if that light *is* flashed, what is it flashed for?'

'Old Grandad said there hadn't been any wrecks on this coast for ages,' said Julian. 'I think that the old man is confused a bit in his mind about that light!'

'But Yan said he'd seen it, too,' said Anne.

'I'm not sure that Yan's as truthful as he could be!' said Julian.

'Why did Grandad say that the light isn't flashed by mortal hands now?' asked George. 'It must be! I can't imagine any other hands working it! He surely doesn't think that his dad is still doing it?'

There was a pause.

'We could easily find out if we popped over to that tower and had a look at it,' said Dick.

There was another pause.

'I thought we said we wouldn't go poking about in anything mysterious,' said Anne.

'This isn't really mysterious,' argued Dick. 'It's just a story an old man remembers, and I really *can't* believe that that light still flashes on a wild stormy night. Grandad must have seen lightning or something. Why don't we settle the matter for good and all and go and explore the old house with the tower?'

'I'd like to,' said George firmly. 'I never was keen on this "Keep away from anything unusual" idea we suddenly had. We've got Timmy with us – we can't possibly come to any harm!'

'All right,' said Anne, with a sigh. 'I give up. We'll go if you want to.'

'Good old Anne,' said Dick, giving her a friendly slap on the back. 'But *you* needn't come, you know. Why don't you stay behind and hear our story when we come back?'

'I will *not*,' said Anne, quite cross. 'I may not want to go as much as you do, but I'm not going to be left out of anything, so don't think it!'

'All right. It's settled then,' said Julian. 'Let's take our chance and go as soon as we can. Tomorrow, perhaps.'

Mrs Penruthlan came to the door and called them. 'Your tea's ready. You must be hungry. Come along indoors.'

The sun suddenly went in. Julian looked up at the sky in surprise.

'Hey, look at those black clouds!' he said. 'There's a storm coming! Well, I thought there might be, it's been so hot all day!'

'A storm!' said George. 'That light flashes on wild and stormy nights! Oh, Julian, do you think it'll flash tonight? Can't we – *can't* we go and see?'

7 *Out in the night*

Before the children had finished their tea, the big kitchen was quite dark. Thunder clouds had moved up from the west, gathering together silently, frowning and sinister. Then, from far off, came the first rumble of thunder.

The little Scottie came and cowered against Mrs Penruthlan's legs. He hated storms. The farmer's wife comforted him, and her big husband gave a little unexpected snort of laughter. He said something that sounded like 'oose'.

'He's *not* as timid as a mouse,' said his wife, who was really skilled at interpreting her husband's strange noises. 'He just doesn't like the thunder. He never did. He can sleep with us in our room tonight.'

There were a few more sounds from Mr Penruthlan to which his wife listened anxiously. 'All right, if you have to get up and see to Jenny the horse in the night, I'll see Benny doesn't bark the house down,' she said. She turned to the children. 'Don't worry if you hear him barking,' she said. 'It'll only be Mr Penruthlan stirring.'

The thunder crashed and rumbled again, this time a little nearer, and then lightning flashed. Then down came the rain. How it poured! It rattled and clattered on the roof in enormous drops, and then settled down into a steady downpour.

The four children got out their cards and played games by the light of the oil lamp. There was no electricity at Tremannon. Timmy sat with his head on George's knee. He didn't mind the thunder but he didn't particularly like it.

'Well, I think we'd better go to bed,' said Julian at last.

He knew that the Penruthlans liked to go to bed early because they got up so early, and as they wouldn't go upstairs until after the children did, Julian made sure that they, too, went early.

They said goodnight and went up to their bare little rooms. The windows were still open and the small curtains drawn back, so that the hills, lit now and again by lightning, showed up clearly. The children went and stood there, watching. They all loved a storm, especially Dick. There was something powerful and very majestic about this kind of storm, sweeping over hills and sea, rumbling all around, and tearing the sky in half with flashes of lightning.

'Julian, can we go up to that place the shepherd showed us and see if the light flashes tonight?' said George. 'You only laughed when I asked you before.'

'Well, I laugh again!' said Julian. 'Of course not! We'd be drenched, and I don't fancy being out in this lightning on those exposed hills, either.'

'All right,' said George. 'Anyway, I don't feel *quite* such an urge to go now that it's so pitch-dark.'

'Just as well,' said Julian. 'Come on, Dick, let's go to bed.'

The storm went on for some time, rumbling all around the hills again, as if it were going around in a circle. The girls fell asleep, but the boys tossed about, feeling hot and sticky.

'Dick,' said Julian, suddenly, 'let's get up and go out. It's stopped raining. Let's go and see if that light is flashing tonight. It should be just the night for it, according to Grandad.'

'Right,' said Dick, and sat up, feeling for his

clothes. 'I can't go to sleep, even though I felt really sleepy when I undressed.'

They pulled on as few clothes as possible, for the night was still thundery and hot. Julian took his torch and Dick hunted for his.

'Got it,' he said at last. 'Are you ready? Come on, then. Let's tiptoe past the Penruthlans' door, or we may wake that Scottie dog! He's sleeping there tonight, don't forget.'

They tiptoed along the passage, past the Penruthlans' door and down the stairs. One stair creaked alarmingly, and they stopped in dismay, wondering if Ben the Scottie would break out into a storm of barking.

But he didn't. Good! Down they went again, switching on their torches to see the way. They came to the bottom of the stairs.

'Shall we go out by the front door or back door, Ju?' whispered Dick.

'Back,' said Julian. 'The front door's so heavy to open. Come on.'

So they went down the passage to the back door that led out from the kitchen. It was locked and bolted, but the two boys opened it without too much noise.

They stepped out into the night. The rain had now stopped, but the sky was still dark and clouded. The thunder rumbled away in the distance. A wind had got up and blew coolly against the boys' faces.

'Nice cool breeze,' whispered Dick. 'Now – do we go through the farmyard? Is that the shortest way to the stile we have to climb over into that first field?'

'Yes, I think so,' said Julian.

They made their way across the silent farmyard, where, in the daytime, such a lot of noise went on, clucking, quacking, grunting, clip-clopping, and shouting!

Now it was dark and deserted. They passed the barns and the stables. A little 'hrrrrrrumphing' came from one of the stables.

'That's Jenny, the horse that's not well,' said Julian, stopping. 'Let's just have a look at her and see if she's all right. She was lying down feeling very sorry for herself when I saw her last.'

They flashed their torch over the top half of the stable door, which was pulled back to let in air. They looked in with interest.

Jenny was no longer lying down. She was

standing up, munching something. She must be all right again! She whinnied to the two boys.

They left her and went on. They came to the stile and climbed over. The rain began drizzling again, and if the boys hadn't had their torches with them they wouldn't have been able to see a step in front of them, it was so dark.

'Hey, Ju – did you hear that?' said Dick, stopping suddenly.

'No. What?' said Julian, listening.

'Well, it sounded like a cough,' said Dick.

'One of the sheep,' suggested Julian. 'I heard one old sheep coughing just like Uncle Quentin does sometimes, sort of hollow and mournful.'

'No. It wasn't a sheep,' said Dick. 'Anyway, there aren't any in this field.'

'You imagined it,' said Julian. 'I bet there's nobody idiotic enough to be out on a night like this, except us!'

They went on cautiously over the field. The thunder began again, a little nearer. Then came a flash, and again the thunder. Dick stopped dead once more and clutched Julian's arm.

'There's somebody a good way in front of us, the lightning just lit him up for half a second. He was climbing over that stile, the one we're making for. Who do you think it is on a night like this?'

'He's going the same way that we are,' said Julian. 'Well, I suppose if we saw *him* he probably saw *us*!'

'Not unless he was looking backwards,' said Dick. 'Come on, let's see where he's going.'

They went on cautiously towards the stile. They came to it and climbed over. And then a hand suddenly clutched hold of Dick's shoulder!

He almost jumped out of his skin! The hand gripped him so hard and so fiercely that Dick shouted in pain and tried to wriggle away from the powerful grip.

Julian felt a hand lunge at him, too, but dodged and pressed himself into the hedge. He switched off his torch at once and stood still, his heart thumping.

'Let me go!' shouted Dick, wriggling like an eel.

His shirt was almost torn off his back in his struggles. He kicked out at the man's ankles and for one moment his captor loosened his grasp. That was enough for Dick. He ripped himself away and left his shirt in the man's hand!

He ran up the lane into which the stile had led and flung himself under a bush in the darkness, panting. He heard his captor coming along, muttering, and Dick pressed himself farther into the bush. A torchlight swept the ground near him, but missed him.

Dick waited till the footsteps had gone and then crawled out. He went quietly down the lane.

'Julian!' he whispered, and jumped as a voice answered almost in his ear, just above his head!

'I'm here. Are you all right?'

Dick looked up into the darkness of a tree, but could see nothing.

'I've dropped my torch somewhere,' he said. 'Where are you, Ju? Up in the tree?'

A hand groped out and felt his head.

'Here I am, on the first branch,' said Julian. 'I hid in the hedge first and then climbed up here. I daren't put on my torch in case that man's anywhere around and sees it.'

'He's gone up the lane,' said Dick. 'He nearly wrenched my shoulder off. Half my shirt's gone! Who was he? Did you see?'

'No. I didn't,' said Julian, clambering down.

'Let's find your torch before we go home. It's too good to lose. It must be by that stile.'

They went to look. Julian still didn't like to put on his torch, so it was more a question of *feeling* for Dick's torch, not looking! Dick suddenly trod on it and picked it up thankfully.

'Listen, there's that man coming back again. I'm sure!' said Dick. 'I heard the same dry little cough! What shall we do?'

'Well, I don't now feel like going up to the shepherd's hill to see if that light is flashing from the tower,' said Julian. 'Let's hide and follow this man to see where he goes. I don't think anyone who's wandering out tonight can be up to any good.'

'Yes. Good idea,' said Dick. 'Squash into the hedge again. Oh no, there are nettles here! Just my luck.'

The footsteps came nearer, and the cough came again.

'I seem to know that cough,' whispered Dick.

'Shh!' said Julian.

The man came up to the stile, and they heard him climbing over it. After a short time both boys followed cautiously. They couldn't hear the man's footsteps across the grass, but the sky had cleared a little and they could just make out a moving shadow ahead of them.

They followed him at a distance, holding their breath whenever they kicked against a stone or cracked a twig beneath their feet. Now and again they heard the cough.

'He's making for the farm,' whispered Julian. He could just see the outline of the big barns against the sky. 'Do you think he's one of the labourers? They live in cottages around about.'

The man came to the farmyard and walked through it, trying to make as little sound as possible. The boys followed. He went around the barns and into the little garden that Mrs Penruthlan tended herself. Still the boys followed.

Around to the front door went the man, and the boys held their breath. Was he going to burgle the farmhouse? They tiptoed nearer. There came the sound of a soft click, and then of bolts being shot home! After that there was silence.

'He's gone in,' said Julian in amazement.

'Don't you know who it was? Can't you guess now?' said Dick. 'We both ought to have known when we heard that cough! It was Mr Penruthlan!

No wonder he almost dislocated my shoulder with his strong hand!'

'*Mr Penruthlan* – yes, you're right,' said Julian, astonished, almost forgetting to speak in a whisper. 'We didn't notice that the front door was undone because we went out the back way. So it was him we followed. How silly! But what was he doing out on the hills? He didn't go to see the horse, she wasn't ill.'

'Perhaps he likes a walk at night,' suggested Dick. 'Come on, let's go in ourselves. I feel a bit chilly with practically no shirt on!'

They crept around to the back door. It was still open, thank goodness! They went inside, bolted and locked it, and tiptoed upstairs. They heaved sighs of relief when they were safely in their room again.

'Switch on your torch, Julian, and see if my shoulder is bruised,' said Dick. 'It feels really painful.'

Julian flashed his torch on Dick's shoulder. He gave a low whistle. 'You've got a wonderful bruise all down your right shoulder. He must have given you a nasty wrench.'

'He did,' said poor Dick. 'Well, I can't say

we had a very successful time. We followed our host through the night, got caught by him, and then followed him all the way back here. *Not* very clever!'

'Well, never mind, I bet no light flashed in that tower,' said Julian, getting into bed. 'We haven't lost much by not going all the way to see!'

8 Here come the Barnies!

The two boys looked curiously at Mr Penruthlan the next morning. It seemed strange to think of their little adventure the night before with him, and *he* didn't even know it was them he'd tried to catch! He gave the strange little dry cough again, and Julian nudged Dick and grinned.

Mrs Penruthlan was beaming at the head of the breakfast table as usual. 'The storm soon died down, didn't it?'

Mr Penruthlan got up, said 'Ah, ock, oooh!' or something that sounded like that, and went out.

'What did he say?' asked Anne curiously.

She could *not* think how anyone could possibly understand Mr Penruthlan's extraordinary speech. Julian had said that he thought he must talk in shorthand!

'He said he might not be back for lunch,' said Mrs Penruthlan. 'I hope he'll get some somewhere. He had his breakfast at half past six, and that's very early. I'm glad he came in and had a cup of your breakfast tea now. The poor man had a very bad night, I'm sorry to say.'

The boys pricked up their ears. 'What happened?' asked Julian at once.

'Oh, he had to get up and go and spend two hours with poor Jenny,' said Mrs Penruthlan. 'I woke when he left, but luckily Benny didn't bark, and it wasn't till two hours later he came back, he'd been sitting with the horse all that time, poor man.'

Julian and Dick didn't feel at all sympathetic. They knew exactly where Mr Penruthlan had been, not with the horse, that was certain! Anyway, Jenny hadn't been ill when they had looked at her in the night. What a lot of lies!

They were puzzled. Why should Mr Penruthlan deceive his wife and tell her what wasn't true? What had he been doing that he didn't even want *her* to know?

They told the girls everything immediately after breakfast, when they went to pick currants, raspberries and plums for a fruit salad. Anne and George listened in surprise.

'You never told us you were going,' said George,

reproachfully. 'I'd like to have come with you.'

'I always thought Mr Penruthlan looked sort of strange and – and *scary*,' said Anne. 'I'm sure he's up to no good. What a pity. His wife is so nice.'

They went on picking the endless redcurrants. Anne suddenly got the feeling that somebody was hiding somewhere near. She looked around uncomfortably. Yes, there was someone in the tall raspberry canes, she was sure! She watched.

It was Yan, of course. She might have guessed! He flashed his smile at her and came towards her. He liked Anne best of all! He held out his hand.

'No, I've got no sweets,' said Anne. 'How did you get on last night in the storm, Yan? Were you frightened?'

Yan shook his head. Then he came nearer and spoke softly.

'I saw the light last night!'

Anne stared at him, astonished. What light?

'You don't mean – the light that flashes in that old hidden tower?' she said.

He nodded. Anne went quickly to Julian and Dick, who were picking redcurrants and eating just about as many as they put into the basket!

'Julian! Dick! Yan says he saw that light

flashing last night, the one in the tower!'

'Oh!' said the boys together. They turned to Yan, who had followed Anne. 'You saw that light?' said Julian.

Yan nodded. 'Big light. Very big,' he said. 'Like – like a fire.'

'Shining from the tower?' said Dick, and Yan nodded again.

'Did your grandad see it?' asked Dick.

Yan nodded. 'He saw it, too.'

'Are you telling the truth?' demanded Julian, wondering how far he could believe Yan.

Yan nodded again.

'What time was this?' asked Dick.

But that Yan couldn't tell him. He had no watch, and if he had had, he wouldn't have been able to use it. He couldn't tell the time.

'Oh no!' said Julian to Dick. 'We missed it. If Yan's telling the truth we'd have seen that light last night.'

'Yes. Well, we'll go tonight and watch for it,' said Dick, determined. 'It's a wild enough day, all wind and scurrying clouds. If that light is used at night in weather like this, we'll be able to see it again. But I can't understand why the Wreckers' tower should be used nowadays. No ship would take any notice of an odd light like that when they've got the lighthouse signalling hard all the time!'

'I'll come, too,' nodded Yan, who had overheard this.

'No, you won't,' said Julian. 'You stay with Grandad. He'll wonder where you are if you're not there.'

It began to rain.

'Oh no!' said George. 'I hope the weather hasn't changed. It's been so gorgeous. It's quite cold today with this tearing wind. Come on, let's go in, Anne. We've got enough now to feed an army, I should think!'

They all went in, just as the rain came down properly. Mrs Penruthlan greeted them in excitement.

'The Barnies want our barn for tomorrow night!' she said. 'They're giving their first show in our barn, and after that they go to another place. Would you like to help clear out the barn and get ready?'

'Definitely!' said Julian. 'We'll go now. There's a lot of stuff to clear out. Where shall we put it? In the other barn?'

The Barnies arrived in about twenty minutes and went straight to the barn, which they had been lent several times before for their shows. They were pleased to see the children and were glad of their help.

They were no longer in fancy dress, as they had been when the children had seen them on the Sunday evening. They were almost all dressed in jeans, ready for the hard work of clearing the barn and setting up a simple stage and background.

Julian caught sight of a horse's head being carried in by a little nimble man who pranced along with it comically.

'What's that for?' he said. 'Oh, is that Clopper's head? The horse that can sit down and cross its legs?'

'That's right,' said the little man. 'I'm in charge of it. Never let it out of my sight! Guv'nor's orders!'

'Who's the Guv'nor?' asked Julian. 'The man over there?'

He nodded to a grim-faced man who was supervising the moving of some bales of straw.

'That's him,' said the little man with a grin. 'His lordship himself! What do you think of my horse?'

Julian looked at the horse's head. It was beautifully made and had a very comical look in its eye. Its mouth could open and shut, and so could its big eyes.

'I'm only the hind legs,' said the little man regretfully. 'But I work his tail, too. Mr Binks over there is his front legs, and works his head, the horse's head, I mean. You should see Clopper when he performs! There isn't a horse like him in the world. He can do everything short of fly!'

'Where are his back and front legs – and – er – his body?' asked Dick, coming up and looking with great interest at the horse's head.

'Over there,' said the little man. 'By the way, my name's Sid. What's yours, and how is it you're here?'

Julian introduced himself and Dick, and explained that they were helping because they were staying at the farm. He caught hold of a bale of straw, thinking it was about time he did some work.

'Like to give me a hand?' he asked.

Sid shook his head.

'Sorry. Orders are I'm not to put this horse's head down anywhere. Where I go, it goes! Clopper and I are quite attached to one another!'

'Why? Is it so valuable?' asked Dick.

'It's not so much that,' said Sid. 'It's just that Clopper's so popular, you know. And he's important. You see, whenever we think the show's flopping a bit, we bring Clopper on, and then we get the laughs and the claps, and the audience is in a good mood. Oh, Clopper's saved the show many times. He's a really good horse.'

Mr Binks came up. He was bigger than Sid and much stronger. He grinned at the two boys.

'Admiring Clopper?' he said. 'Did Sid tell you about the time Clopper's head dropped off the wagon and we didn't miss him till we were miles away? What a state the Guv'nor was in! Said we couldn't give a show without Clopper, and nearly gave us all the sack!'

'We're important, we are,' said Sid, throwing out his chest and doing a funny little strut with the horse's head in front of him. 'Me and Binks and Clopper – there'd be no show without us!'

'Don't you put that horse down even for a

moment,' warned Mr Binks. 'The Guv'nor's got his eye on you, Sid. Look, he's calling you.'

Sid went over to the Guv'nor, looking rather alarmed. He carried the horse's head safely under his arm.

The grim-faced man said a few sharp words and Sid nodded. Julian went up to him when he came back.

'Let me feel how heavy the horse's head is,' he said. 'I've often wondered, when I've seen something like this on the stage.'

Sid immediately put the horse under his other arm, and glared at Julian, looking around quickly to see if the Guv'nor had heard.

'That's a stupid thing to ask me,' he said. 'After I've told you I'm not allowed to put the horse down! And didn't the Guv'nor just this minute say to me "Keep away from those kids, you know what tricks they're up to. They'll have that horse away from you if you're not careful." See? Do you want me to lose my job?'

Julian laughed. 'Don't be silly. You wouldn't lose your job for that! When are you and Mr Binks going to do a bit of practice? We want to see you!'

'Oh well, we could manage that all right,' said Sid, calming down. 'Here, Binks. Bit of practice wanted. Get the legs.'

Binks and Sid went to a cleared space in the big barn and proceeded to clothe themselves in the horse's canvas skin and legs. Sid showed the boys how he worked the tail with one of his hands when he wanted to.

Binks put on the head and the front legs. His head only went into the neck of the horse, no farther. He was able to use his hands for pulling strings to open the horse's mouth and work its rolling eyes.

Sid got his legs in the horse's back legs, bent over and put his head and arms over towards Binks, so making the horse's back. Somebody came up and zipped up the two halves of the horse's 'skin'.

'Oh! What a great horse!' said Dick, delighted.

It looked a lively, comical, extremely supple beast, and the two men inside at once proceeded to make it do ridiculous things. It marched – left-right, left-right, left-right. It did a little tap-dance with its front feet, which then remained perfectly still, and then the back feet did the same little tap-dance.

The back feet got themselves entangled and fell over, and the horse's head looked around at itself in astonishment.

All four children were now watching, and Yan was peering in at the door. They roared with laughter at the ridiculous horse.

It took its tail in its mouth and marched round and round itself. It stood up on its hind legs only. It jumped like a kangaroo, and made strange noises. The whole company stood and watched and even the grim-faced Guv'nor had to smile.

Then it sat down on its hind legs and crossed its front ones in the air, looking around comically. It then gave an enormous yawn that showed dozens of large teeth.

'Oh, don't do any more!' cried Anne, who was weak with laughing. 'Don't! Oh, I can see how important you are, Clopper! You'll be the best part of the show!'

It was a mad, happy morning, for the Barnies were full of chatter and jokes and laughter. Sid and Binks took off their horse garments, and then Sid went about as before, the horse's head, grinning comically, tucked safely under his arm.

Mrs Penruthlan called the children in to lunch. Yan ran after Julian, and caught hold of his arm.

'I saw that light,' he said, urgently. 'Come and see it tonight. Don't forget. I saw that light!'

Julian *had* forgotten it in the excitement of the morning. He grinned down at the small boy.

'All right, all right. I won't forget. We're coming along tonight, but you're not coming, Yan, so get that out of your head! Look, here's a sweet for you. Now, go!'

9 The light in the tower

By the end of the day the big barn was completely transformed! It had been cleared of all straw, sacks of corn, bags of fertiliser and odd machines that had been stored in it. It looked enormous now, and the Barnies were very pleased with it.

'We've been here plenty of times,' they told the children. 'It's the best barn in the district. We don't get the best audience, though, because it's a lonely spot here, and there are only two villages near enough to send people to see us. Still, we have a good time, and Mrs Penruthlan gives us a wonderful supper afterwards!'

'I bet she does!' said Dick, grinning. 'I bet that's why you come to this lonely spot, too, to taste Mrs Penruthlan's cooking. I don't blame you. I'd come a good few miles myself!'

A stage had been set up, made of long boards, supported on barrels. A backcloth had been unrolled and hung over the wooden wall of the barn at the back of the stage. It showed a country scene, and had been painted by the company themselves, bit by bit.

'That's my bit,' said Sid, showing Dick a horse standing in one of the fields painted on the backcloth. 'I had to put Clopper in! See him?'

The Barnies had plenty of scenery, which they were used to changing several times during their performance. This was all home-made too, and they were very proud of it, especially some that represented a castle with a tower.

The tower reminded the boys of the one Yan had said he'd seen flashing a light the night before. They looked at one another secretly, and Julian nodded slightly. They would certainly watch to see that light themselves. Then they'd know for certain whether Grandad and Yan were telling the truth.

Julian wondered if they would have to look out for Mr Penruthlan again that night. Jenny the horse was better now, if she had ever been ill, and was out in the fields again. So Mr Penruthlan had no excuse for creeping about the countryside at night again!

Neither of the boys could *imagine* what had

taken him out the night before, on such a wild night too! Was he meeting somebody? He hadn't had time to go up to see the shepherd about anything, and there wouldn't have been much point in that anyway. He'd seen Grandad in the morning already.

Mrs Penruthlan came to see the barn now that it was almost ready for the show the next night. She looked red and excited. This was a wonderful time for her, the Barnies in her barn, the villagers all coming up the next night, a big supper to be held afterwards. What an excitement!

She was very busy in her kitchen, cooking, cooking, cooking! Her enormous larder was already full of very appetising-looking pies, tarts, hams and cheeses. The children took turns at looking into it and sniffing in delight. Mrs Penruthlan laughed at them and shooed them out.

'You'll have to help me tomorrow,' she said. 'Shelling peas, scraping potatoes, stringing beans, picking currants and raspberries, and you'll find hundreds of wild strawberries in the copse too, which can go to add a flavour to the fruit salad.'

'We'll love to help,' said Anne. 'All this is great fun! But surely you aren't going to do all the supper alone, Mrs Penruthlan?'

'Oh, one or two of the villagers will stay behind to help me serve it,' said the farmer's wife, who looked as happy as could be in the midst of so much hard work. 'Anyway, I'll be up at five o'clock tomorrow morning. I'll have plenty of time!'

'You'd better go to bed early tonight then!' said George.

'We all will,' said Mrs Penruthlan. 'We'll be up early and in bed late tomorrow, and we'll need some sleep tonight. It's no trouble to get Mr Penruthlan to bed early. He's always ready to go!'

The children felt sure he'd be ready to go early that night because he'd spent so much time out in the storm the night before! Julian and Dick were tired too, but they were determined to go up to the shepherd's hill and find the place where they could watch and see if that light really did flash out!

They had tea as usual, at which Mr Penruthlan was present. He ate solidly and solemnly, not saying a word except something that sounded like 'Ooahah, ooh.'

'Well, I'm glad you like the pie, Mr Penruthlan,' said his wife. 'Though I say it myself, it's a good one.'

It really was wonderful the way she understood her husband's speech. It was also very strange to hear her speak to her husband as if he was someone to whom she had to be polite, and call Mister! Anne wondered if she called him Mr Penruthlan when they were alone together. She looked at him earnestly. What a dark giant he was – and how he ate!

He looked up and saw Anne watching him. He nodded at her and said 'Ah! Oooh, ock, ukker.' It might have been a foreign language for all Anne could understand! She looked startled and didn't know what to say.

'Now, Mr Penruthlan, don't you tease the child!' said his wife. 'She doesn't know what to answer. Do you, Anne?'

'Well – I – er – I didn't really catch what he said,' said Anne, going scarlet.

'There now, Mr Penruthlan – see how badly you talk without your teeth in!' said the farmer's wife scoldingly. 'Haven't I told you you should wear your teeth when you want to make conversation! *I* understand you all right, but others don't. It must sound just a mumble to them!'

Mr Penruthlan frowned and muttered something. The children all stared at him, dumbfounded to hear that he had no teeth. HOW did he manage to eat all he did, then? He seemed to chew and munch and crunch, and yet he had no teeth!

'So that's why he speaks so oddly,' thought Dick, amused. 'But imagine eating as much as he does, with no teeth in his head! What would he eat if he *had* got all his teeth?'

Mrs Penruthlan changed the conversation because it was clear that her husband was annoyed with her. She talked brightly about the Barnies.

'That horse Clopper! You wait till you see him prance on to the stage, and fall off it. You'll see Mr Penruthlan almost fall out of his seat he laughs so much. He loves that horse. He's seen it a dozen times, and it tickles him to death.'

'I think it's really funny too,' said Julian. 'I've always thought I'd like to put on an act like that at our end-of-term concert at school. Dick and I could do it all right. I wish Sid and

Mr Binks would let us try.'

The meal was finished at last. Most of the dishes were empty, and Mrs Penruthlan looked pleased.

'There now – you've done really well,' she said. 'That's what I like to see, people finishing up everything put before them.'

'It's easy when it's food *you* put before us,' said George. 'Isn't it, Timmy? I bet Timmy wishes he lived here always, Mrs Penruthlan! I'm sure he keeps telling your dogs how lucky they are!'

After the washing up, in which everyone but Mr Penruthlan helped, they went to sit down for a while, and read. But the farmer kept giving such enormous yawns that he set everyone else yawning too, and Mrs Penruthlan began to laugh.

'Come on, to bed, all of you!' she said. 'I've never heard so many yawns in my life! Poor Mr Penruthlan. He's tired out with sitting up with Jenny the horse half the night.'

The children exchanged glances. They knew better!

Everyone went up to bed, and the children laughed to hear Mr Penruthlan still yawning loudly in his room. Julian looked out of his window. It was a dark, blustery night, with sudden spurts of sharp rain. The wind howled and Julian almost thought he could hear the great waves crashing on the rocks in the nearest coves! How enormous they would be in this wind!

'A good night for Wreckers, if there were any nowadays!' he said to Dick. 'Not much chance for any ship that went too near those coves tonight! They'd be on the rocks, and dashed to pieces in half an hour! The beach would be strewn with thousands of pieces of wreckage the next day.'

'We'd better wait a bit before we go,' said Dick. 'It's really very early. On a bright sunny evening the hills would still be full of daylight, but this stormy evening is very dark. Let's light our torches and read.'

The wind became even stronger, and grew almost to a gale. It made a howling noise around the old farmhouse, and sounded angry and in pain. Not a very nice night to go out on the hills!

'We'll go now, I think,' said Julian, at last. 'It's quite dark, and getting late. Come on.'

They hadn't undressed, so they went down the

stairs at once, and out of the back door as before, closing it silently behind them. They made their way through the farmyard, not daring to shine their torches till they were well away from the house.

They had had a quick look at the front door, when they had stood in the hall. It was locked and bolted! Mr Penruthlan wasn't out tonight, that was certain.

They walked steadily through the gale, gasping when it caught them full in the face. They each had their warm jumpers on, for it was quite cold, and the wind blew all the time.

Across the fields. Over one stile after another. Across more fields. The boys stopped once or twice to make sure they were right. They were relieved when they came to the great flock of sheep, and knew they must be near the shepherd's hut.

'There's the hut,' whispered Julian, at last. 'You can just see its dark outline. We must go quietly now.'

They stole by the hut. Not a sound came from inside, and no candlelight showed through the cracks. Grandad must be fast asleep! Julian pictured Yan curled up with him on their bed of old sheepskins.

The boys went quietly along. Now, they must make for the spot from which the old tower could be seen, and it must be the *exact* spot, for the tower could be seen from nowhere else.

They couldn't find it, or, if they *had* found it, and were standing on it, they were unable to see the tower far off in the darkness.

'If it didn't happen to be flashing a light, we wouldn't know if we were looking in the right direction or not!' said Julian. 'We'd never see it in the dark. Why didn't we think of that? Somehow I thought we'd see the tower whether it was lit up or not. We're idiots.'

They wandered about a little, continually looking in the direction where they thought the tower should be but saw nothing at all. What a waste of a long walk!

Then Julian suddenly gave an exclamation. 'Who's that? I saw someone there! Who is it?'

Dick jumped. What was this now? Then someone sidled up against them both, and a voice spoke timidly.

'It's me, Yan!'

'You turn up everywhere!' said Julian. 'I suppose you were watching out for us.'

'Yes. Come with me,' said Yan, and tugged at Julian's arm.

The two boys went with him, a few yards to the right, then higher up the hill. Then Yan stopped.

The boys saw the distant light at once. There was no doubt about it at all! It flashed continually, a bit like a small lighthouse light. Each time it flashed they could see the faint outline of the tower.

'It seems to be some kind of signal,' said Julian. 'Flash – flash-flash-flash – flash-flash – flash. How strange. Who's doing it, and why? Surely there are no Wreckers nowadays!'

'Grandad says it's his old dad,' said Yan, in an awed voice.

Julian laughed.

'Don't be silly! All the same, it's a bit of a mystery, isn't it, Dick? *Could* any ship out at sea be deceived and come near to the shore, and be wrecked? It's a wicked night, just the night for great waves to pound a ship to pieces if it came near this coast.'

'Yes. Well, we'll hear tomorrow if there *has* been a wreck,' said Dick soberly. 'I hope there won't be. I can't bear thinking of it, anyway. Surely, *surely* there aren't Wreckers here now!'

'If there are, they'll be creeping down the hidden Wreckers' Way, wherever it is,' said Julian. 'And watching for the ship to crash to pieces. Then they'll collect sacks upon sacks of booty and creep away back.'

Dick felt a chill of horror.

'Shut up, Ju!' he said, sharply. 'Don't talk like that. Now, what are we going to do about that light?'

'I'll tell you,' said Julian, firmly. 'We're going to find that tower and see what's going on. That's what we're going to do! And as soon as we can too, maybe tomorrow!'

10 Getting ready for the show

Julian and Dick watched the light for a little longer, and then turned to go back to the farm. The wind was so strong and so cold that even on that summer's night they found themselves shivering.

'I'm glad you found us, Yan,' said Dick, putting an arm around the small, shivering boy. 'Thanks for your help. We're going to explore the old tower. Would you like to show us the way to it?'

Yan shivered all the more, from fright as much as cold.

'No. I'm frightened,' he said. 'I'm frightened of that tower now.'

'All right, Yan,' said Dick. 'You needn't come. It is pretty strange, I must admit. Now, go back to your hut.'

Yan shot off in the dark like a scared rabbit. The boys made their way home, not very cautiously, for they felt sure they were the only people out at night. But when they came to the farmyard they saw something that made them stop suddenly.

'There's a light in the big barn!' whispered Dick. 'It's gone, no, there it is again. It's somebody with a torch, flashing it on and off. Who is it?'

'One of the Barnies, perhaps,' whispered back Julian. 'Let's go and see. We know the Barnies are sleeping in the nearby sheds tonight.'

They tiptoed to the barn and looked through a crack. They saw nothing at first. Then a torch flashed, shedding its light on some of the properties of the Barnies, stacked in a corner, scenery, dresses, coats, and other things.

'Somebody's going through the pockets!' said Julian, indignantly. 'Look at that! A thief!'

'Who is it?' said Dick. 'One of the Barnies pickpocketing?'

For a moment or two the torch lit up the back of the intruder's hand in the barn, and the boys stifled an exclamation. They knew that hand! It was covered with black hairs almost as thick as fur!

'Mr Penruthlan!' whispered Dick. 'Yes, I see it's him now. Look at his enormous shadow. What's he doing? He must be mad, walking around at night on the hills, creeping into the barn, going through pockets. Look what he's doing now! Looking in the drawers of that chest the Barnies are going to use in one of their scenes. Yes, he's mad!'

Julian felt very uncomfortable. He didn't like spying on his host like this. What a strange man he was! He told lies, he crept about at night, he went through people's pockets. Yes, he must be mad! Did Mrs Penruthlan know? She couldn't know, or she'd be unhappy, and she really seemed the most cheerful happy person in the world!

'Come on,' said Julian, in Dick's ear. 'He's going through everything! Although what he expects to find in the Barnies' stage clothes and properties, I don't know. He's strange! Come on, I really don't want to spot him taking something, stealing it. It'd be so awkward if we had to say we saw him stealing.'

They left the barn and went back to the farmhouse, creeping in once more at the back door. They looked at the front door. It was shut, but no longer locked or bolted.

The boys went upstairs, puzzled. What a

strange night! The howling wind, the flashing light, the furtive man in the barn – they didn't know what to make of it!

'Let's wake the girls and tell them,' said Julian. 'I feel as if I can't wait till the morning.'

George was awake and so was Timmy. Timmy had heard them going out, and had lain awake waiting for them to come back. He had stirred and had awakened George. She was waiting to hear a whisper at the door!

'Anne! George! We've got some news!' whispered Julian.

Timmy gave a little welcoming whine and leapt off the bed. Soon Anne was awake, too, and the girls were listening in amazement to the boys' news.

They were almost as surprised to hear about Mr Penruthlan in the barn as to hear about the light actually flashing in the tower.

'So it *was* true what Grandad said, then?' whispered Anne. 'He *had* seen the light again. I do think it's strange, all this. Julian, you don't think we'll hear of a wreck tomorrow, do you? I couldn't bear it!'

'Nor could I,' said George, listening to the wind

howling outside. 'Imagine being wrecked on a night like this, and being dashed on the rocks by those pounding waves. I feel as if we ought to rush off to the coves here and now and see if we can do any rescuing!'

'We wouldn't be much use,' said Dick. 'I doubt if we could even get near the cove on a night like this. The waves would run right up to the road that leads down to it.'

They talked and talked about everything. Then George yawned.

'We'd better stop,' she said. 'We'll never wake up tomorrow morning. We can't go and explore that tower tomorrow, Julian. The Barnies will be here, and we've promised Mrs Penruthlan to help her.'

'It'll have to be next day, then,' said Julian. 'But I'm determined to go. Yan said he wouldn't show us the way. He said he was too frightened!'

'I feel pretty frightened myself,' said George, settling down. 'I'd have jumped out of my skin if I'd seen that light tonight.'

The boys crept back to their room. Soon they were in bed and asleep. The wind still howled around the house, but they didn't hear it.

They were tired out with their long walk over the hills.

Next day was so busy that it was difficult to find time to remember the night's happenings! They were reminded of it by one thing, though!

Mrs Penruthlan was seeing to their breakfast, and making bright conversation as usual. She was never at a loss for words, and chattered all day long either to the children or to the dogs.

'Did you sleep well with that howling gale blowing all night long?' she asked. 'I slept like a top. So did Mr Penruthlan! He told me he never moved all night, he was that tired!'

The children kicked each other under the table, but said nothing. They knew a lot more about her husband's nights than she did!

After that they had very little time to think of anything but picking fruit, podding peas, rushing here and there, carrying things for the Barnies, helping them to put up benches, barrels, boxes and chairs for the audience to sit on, and even mending tears in some of the stage clothes! Anne had offered to sew on a button, and at once found herself overwhelmed with requests to mend this, that and the other!

It was an extremely busy day. Yan appeared as usual and was greeted uproariously by Timmy, of course. All the dogs loved him, but Timmy was really silly with him. Mrs Penruthlan sent Yan on endless errands, which he ran quickly and willingly.

'He's quick enough when he thinks there's some food he's going to share!' she said. So it was 'Fetch this, Yan!', 'Do that, Yan!' all day long.

The Barnies worked hard, too. They had a quick rehearsal in which every single thing went wrong; the Guv'nor raved and raged and stamped, making Anne wonder why they didn't all run away and stay away!

First there was to be a kind of concert party. Then there was to be a play, very heart-rending and melodramatic, with villains and heroes and a heroine who was very harshly treated. But everything came right for her in the end, Anne was relieved to find!

Clopper the horse was to have no definite performance of his own. He just wandered on and off the stage to get laughs and to please everyone, or to fill awkward gaps. There was no doubt he would do this to perfection!

Julian and Dick watched Mr Binks and Sid doing a small rehearsal on their own in a corner of the farmyard. How well those back legs and front legs worked together! How that horse danced, trotted, galloped, marched, fell over, tied itself into knots, sat down, got up, went to sleep, and, in fact, did every comical thing that Sid and Mr Binks could think of. They really were very, very funny.

'Let me try the head on, Mr Binks,' begged Julian. 'Please let me. Just to feel what it's like.'

But it was no good. Sid wouldn't let him. Mr Binks had no say in the matter at all.

'Orders are orders,' said Sid, picking up the head as soon as Mr Binks took it off. 'I don't want to lose my job. The Guv'nor says if this horse's head is mislaid again, I'll be mislaid, too! So hands off Clopper!'

'Do you sleep with Clopper?' asked Dick, curiously. 'Having to take charge of a horse's head all the time must be a bore!'

'You get used to it,' said Sid. 'Yes, I sleep with Clopper. Him and me have our heads on the pillow together. He sleeps sound, does Clopper!'

'He's the best part of the show,' grinned

Julian. 'You'll bring the barn down with Clopper tonight!'

'We always do,' said Mr Binks. 'He's the most important member of the Barnies, and he gets paid the worst. Shame.'

'Yes, back legs and front legs are badly paid,' said Sid. 'They only count as one player, see, so we get half pay. Still, we like the life, so there you are!'

They went off together, Sid carrying the horse's head as usual under his arm. He really was a funny little man, cheery and silly and bright.

Julian suddenly remembered something at lunch-time.

'Mrs Penruthlan,' he said, 'I hope that awful wind didn't cause any wrecks last night, did it?'

The farmer's wife looked surprised. 'No, Julian. Why should it? Ships keep right out to sea around these coasts now. The lighthouse warns them, you know. The only way any ship could come in now would be to nose into one of the coves at full tide, and then she'd have to be very careful of rocks. The fishermen know the rocks as well as they know the backs of their hands, and they come into the coves at times. But no other craft come now.'

Everyone heaved a sigh of relief. The flashing light hadn't caused a wreck last night, then. That was good news! They went on with their meal. Mr Penruthlan was there, eating away as usual, and saying nothing at all. His jaws worked vigorously up and down, and it was impossible to think he had no teeth to chew with. Julian glanced at his hands, covered with black hairs. Yes, he'd seen those hands last night, no doubt about that! Not wielding a knife and fork, but sliding into pockets.

The evening came at last. Everything was ready. A big table was placed in the kitchen, made of strong trestles and boards. Mrs Penruthlan gave the children an enormous white cloth to lay over it. It was bigger than any cloth they had ever seen!

'It's the one I use at harvest-time,' said the farmer's wife, proudly. 'We have a wonderful harvest supper then, on that same table, but we put it out in the big barn because there's not enough room here in the kitchen for all the farm workers. And we clear the table away afterwards and have a dance.'

'Sounds like fun!' said Anne. 'I think people

are lucky to live on a farm. There's always something going on!'

'Town people wouldn't say that!' said Mrs Penruthlan. 'They think the country is a dead-and-alive place, but there's more life about a farm than anywhere else in the world. Farm life's the *real* thing, I always say!'

'It is,' agreed Anne, and the others nodded, too. They had now spread out the snowy-white cloth and it looked lovely.

'That cloth's the real thing, too,' said Mrs Penruthlan. 'It belonged to my great-great-great-grandmother, and it's nearly two hundred years old! As white as ever and not a darn in it! It's seen more harvest suppers than any cloth, and that's the truth!'

The table was laid with plates and knives and forks, cruets and glasses. All the Barnies had been invited, and there were the children, too, of course. One or two of the villagers were staying as well, to help. What a feast they would all have!

The larder was so crammed with food that it was difficult to get into it. Meat pies, fruit pies, hams, pickles, sauces, jam tarts, stewed and fresh fruit, jellies, a great trifle, jugs of cream – there was no end to the things Mrs Penruthlan had got ready. She laughed when she saw the children peering there and gasping.

'You won't get any tea today,' she told them. 'You'll get nothing from lunch till supper, so that you can get up a good appetite and really eat well!'

Nobody minded missing tea with that wonderful supper to come. The excitement grew as the time came near for the show.

'Here come the first villagers!' cried Julian, who was at the barn door to help to sell the tickets. 'It'll soon begin! Roll up, everyone! Best show in the world. Come along in your hundreds! Come along!'

11 The Barnies – and Clopper

When the big barn was full of villagers, and a few more boxes had been fetched for some of the extra children, the noise was tremendous. Everyone was laughing and talking, some of the children were clapping for the show to begin, and the excited farm dogs were yapping and barking at the top of their voices!

Timmy was excited, too. He welcomed everyone with a bark and a vigorous wag. Yan was with him, and George was sure that he was pretending that Timmy was his dog! Yan looked cleaner than usual. Mrs Penruthlan had actually given him a bath!

'You don't come to the show and you don't come to the supper unless you bath yourself,' she threatened. But he wouldn't. He said he was frightened of the bath.

'I'll be drowned in there,' he said, backing away from it hurriedly. It was already half full of water for him!

'Frightened are you!' said Mrs Penruthlan grimly, lifting him up and plunging him into the water, clothes and all. 'Well, you'll be more frightened now! Take your clothes off in the water and I'll wash them in the bath when you're clean.'

Yan screamed the place down as Mrs Penruthlan scrubbed him and soaped him and flannelled him. He felt very much at her mercy, and decided not to annoy her in any way while he was in that dreadful bath!

She washed his ragged trousers and shirt, too, and set them to dry. She wrapped him in an old shawl, and told him to wait till his things dried and then put them on.

'One of these days I'll make you some decent clothes,' she said. 'What a mite of a body you've got. I'll need to feed you up a bit!'

Yan brightened up considerably. Feeding up was the kind of treatment he really liked!

Now he was down in the barn, welcoming everyone with Timmy and feeling quite important. He yelled with delight when he saw his great-grandfather coming along!

'Grandad! You said you were coming, but I didn't believe you. Come on in. I'll find you a chair.'

'And what's come over you, the way you look tonight?' said the old man, puzzled. 'What've you done to yourself?'

'I've had a bath,' said Yan, sounding proud. 'Yes. I took a bath, Grandad.'

Grandad nodded to various people he knew. He had his big old shepherd's crook with him, and he held on to it even when he sat down on a chair.

'Well, Grandad, it must be twenty years since we saw you down here,' said a big, red-faced villager. 'What've you been doing with yourself all these years?'

'Minding my business and minding my sheep,' said Grandad, in his slow, Cornish voice. 'Yes, and it might be twenty years before you see me again, Joe Tremayne. And if you want to know something I'll tell you this. It isn't the show I've come for, it's the supper.'

Everyone roared with laughter, and Grandad looked pleased. Yan looked at him proudly. His grandad was as good as anyone, any day!

'Shh! Shh! Show's going to begin!' said somebody, when they saw the curtain twitching.

At once the talking and shuffling stopped, and all eyes turned to the stage. A faded, rather torn blue curtain was drawn across.

There came a chord from a fiddle behind the scenes, and then a lively tune sounded out. The curtain was drawn back slowly, halting on its rings here and there, and the audience gave a long sigh of delight. They had seen the Barnies many times but they never tired of them.

All the Barnies were on the stage, and the fiddler fiddled away as they struck up a rousing song with a chorus that all the villagers joined in with enthusiasm. Grandad beat time, banging his crook on the floor.

Everything was applauded heartily. Then someone called out loudly: 'Where's Clopper? Where is he?'

And Clopper the horse came shyly on, looking out of the sides of his eyes at the audience, and being so very bashful that Grandad almost fell off his chair with laughing.

The fiddle struck up again and Clopper marched in time to it. It grew quicker, and he ran. It grew quicker still and he galloped, and fell right off the stage.

'Hoo-hoo-hoo-hoo!' roared someone. 'HOO-HOO-HOO-HOO!'

It was such an enormous laugh that everyone turned around. It came from Mr Penruthlan, who was writhing and wriggling in his seat as if he was in great pain. But he was only laughing at Clopper.

Clopper heard the giant of a laugh and put a hoof behind one ear to listen to it. Grandad promptly fell off his seat with joy. Clopper caught his back legs in his front legs and fell over too. There was such a pandemonium of screams and laughs and yells from the delighted audience that it was surprising the roof didn't fall in.

'Off now,' said a firm voice at the side of the stage.

Julian looked to see who it was, as Clopper obediently turned to shuffle off, waving one back leg to the admiring villagers. The voice came from the Guv'nor who was standing where he could watch the whole show in detail. His face was still unsmiling, even after Clopper's antics!

The show was a great success, although it

couldn't have been simpler. The jokes were old, the play acted was even older, the singing was a bit flat, and the dancing not very good, but it was so happy and smiling and idiotic and good-natured that it went with a swing from start to finish.

As for Clopper, it was his evening! Every time his head so much as looked in on the stage, the audience rocked with joy. They would, in fact, have been delighted to have had one actor only, all the evening, and that actor, Clopper, of course. Julian and Dick watched him, fascinated. How they both longed to try on those back and front legs, and put on the head, and do a little 'cloppering' themselves!

'Sid and Binks are really good, aren't they?' said Dick. 'I wish we could get hold of legs and a head and do that act at the Christmas school concert, Ju! We'd bring the house down. Let's ask Sid if we can have a go some time.'

'He won't lend us the head,' said Julian. 'Still, we could do without that, and just try the legs. I bet we could think of some funny things to do, Dick!'

Everybody was sad when the curtain went

across the stage, and the show was over.

'Three cheers for the Barnies!' yelled a child, and the cheering rose to the rafters.

Grandad waved his crook too vigorously and hit a very large farmer on the back of his neck.

'Now, Grandad!' said the farmer, rubbing his neck, 'are you trying to pick a fight with me? No, no, I'd be afraid to take you on. You'd get me by my hind leg with that crook like you do your sheep, and down I'd go!'

Grandad was delighted. He hadn't had such an evening for forty years! Maybe fifty. And now for that supper. That was what he'd really come for. He'd show some of these sixty-year-old youngsters how to eat!

The villagers went home, talking and laughing. Two or three of the women stayed on to help. The Barnies didn't bother to change out of their acting clothes, but came into the kitchen as they were, grease-paint running down their cheeks in the heat. The barn had got very hot with so many people packed in close together.

The children were delighted with everything. They had laughed so much at Clopper that they felt quite weak. The play had amused them too, with its sighings and groanings and threats and tears and stridings around. Now they were more than ready for their supper!

The Barnies crowded around the loaded table, cracking jokes, complimenting Mrs Penruthlan, smacking everyone on the back, and generally behaving like a lot of schoolchildren out for a treat. Julian looked around at them all. What a cheerful lot! He looked for the Guv'nor. Surely for once he too would be smiling and cheerful.

But he wasn't there. Julian looked and looked again. No, he definitely wasn't there.

'Where's the Guv'nor?' he asked Sid, who was sitting next to him.

'The Guv'nor? Oh, he's sitting in solitary state in the barn,' said Sid, attacking an enormous slice of meat pie laced with hard-boiled eggs. 'He never eats with us, not even after a show. Keeps himself to himself, he does! He'll be having a whacking great tray of food all on his own. Suits me all right! I never did get on with the Guv'nor.'

'Where's Clopper – the horse's head, I mean?' asked Julian. He couldn't see it beside Sid anywhere. 'Is it under the table?'

'No. The Guv'nor's got it tonight. Said he

wasn't going to have it rolled about under the table, or have jelly or gravy dropped all over it,' said Sid, taking six large pickled onions. 'Mrs Penruthlan is a wonder! Why don't I marry someone like her, instead of getting thinner and thinner inside Clopper's back legs?'

Julian laughed. He wondered who was going to take the Guv'nor's tray into the barn. He noticed that Mrs Penruthlan was getting one ready, and he went over to her.

'Is that for the Guv'nor?' he asked. 'Shall I take it for you?'

'Oh, thank you, Julian,' said the busy farmer's wife, gratefully. 'Here it is, and ask Dick to carry in a bottle and a glass for him, will you? There's no more room on the tray.'

So Julian and Dick together went out to the barn with the food and drink. The wind still blew strongly and rain was beginning to fall again.

'There's no one here,' said Julian, looking around. He set down the tray, puzzled. Then he saw a note pinned on the curtain. He went to read it.

'Back in an hour,' he read. 'Gone for a walk. The Guv'nor.'

'Oh well, we'll leave the tray then,' said Julian.

He and Dick were just turning to go when they caught sight of something, the back and front legs of Clopper the horse! They stopped, each with the same thought in his mind.

'Everyone at supper! The Guv'nor gone for an hour. Nobody would know if we tried on the legs!'

They looked at one another, and read each other's mind. 'Let's have a go at being Clopper!'

'Come on, quick,' said Julian. 'You be the back legs and I'll be the front ones. Quick!'

They got into them hurriedly, and Julian managed to do up most of the zip. But it wasn't right without the head. Had the Guv'nor taken it with him? Surely not? It would be safe in the barn.

'There it is, on that chair under the shawl,' said Dick, and they galloped over to get it.

Julian picked it up. It was heavier than he'd imagined. He looked inside it to see how far his head went in it, wondering how to work the eyes and mouth.

He put his hand inside, and scrabbled about. A

lid fell open in the side of the neck, and out came some cigarettes, scattering over the floor.

'Oh no!' said Julian. 'I didn't know Mr Binks kept his cigarettes in Clopper. Pick them up, Dick, and I'll put them back. Thanks.'

He put the cigarettes back in the little space, and shut the lid on them. Then he put the head carefully over his own. It felt extremely strange.

'There are eye-holes in the neck,' he said to Dick. 'That's how Mr Binks knew where he was going. I kept wondering why he didn't bump into things more than he did! Now – I'm ready. The head seems to be on firmly. I'll count – one-two, one-two – and we'll walk in time. Don't let's start any funny tricks till we're used to Clopper. Does my voice sound funny inside the neck?'

'*Very* strange,' said Dick, who was now bending over so that his back made the horse's back, and his arms were around Julian's waist. 'Hey, what's that?'

'Someone's coming, it's the Guv'nor coming back!' said Julian in alarm. 'Quick, gallop out of the door before we're caught.'

And so, to the Guv'nor's enormous surprise, Clopper galloped very clumsily out of the barn door just as he was coming in, almost knocking him over. At first he didn't realise it was Clopper, then he let out a loud roar and gave chase.

'I can't *see*,' panted poor Julian. 'Where am I going? Oh thank goodness, it's an empty stable! Quick, let's unzip ourselves, and you'll have to take this head off for me, I can't manage it myself.'

But then disaster struck! The zip got stuck and wouldn't come undone. The boys tugged and pulled but it wasn't any use. It looked as if they'd have to be Clopper for the rest of the evening!

12 *A trip to the tower*

'Bother this zip!' said Julian, desperately. 'It's got *absolutely* stuck! It's so difficult for us to undo it from the inside of the horse. Oh, this head. I *must* get it off.'

He pushed at the head but somehow or other it had got wedged on him, and Julian felt that short of pulling his own head off he'd never get Clopper's off!

The horse sat down, exhausted, looking a very strange shape. Julian leaned the head against the wall of the stable and panted. 'I'm so *hot*,' he complained. 'Dick, for goodness' sake think of something. We'll have to get help. But I daren't go back to the barn because of the Guv'nor, and we can't go into the kitchen like this. Everyone'd have a fit, and Sid and Mr Binks would be furious with us.'

'I think we were idiots to try this,' said Dick, pulling viciously at the zip again. 'Ugh! What use are zips, I'd like to know. I'm so uncomfortable. Can't you get in some other position, Ju? I seem to be standing on my head or something.'

'Let's go and scout around the kitchen,' said Julian trying to get up.

Dick tried to get up too, but they both fell down on top of one another. They tried again and this time stood up rather shakily.

'It's not as easy as it looks, is it, to be a two-man horse,' said Julian. 'I wish I could get these eye-holes in the right place. I'm absolutely blind!'

However, he managed to adjust them at last, and the two boys made their way cautiously and clumsily out of the stable. They went carefully over the farmyard, Julian counting one-two, one-two, under his breath so that they walked in time with one another.

They came to the kitchen door and debated whether to try and catch someone's attention without going in. There was a fairly large window nearby, open because of the warmth of the kitchen. Julian decided to take a look through to see if George or Anne were anywhere near. If so, he could call them outside.

But he reckoned without the clumsiness of the big head! It knocked against the window-frame, and everyone looked up. There were shrieks at once.

'A horse! Farmer Penruthlan, one of your horses is loose!' cried a villager who was helping with the supper. 'He looked in at the window!'

The farmer went out at once. Julian and Dick backed hurriedly away and trotted in very good style over the farmyard. Where now? The farmer saw their moving figure in the darkness and went after them.

Trot-trot-trot went the horse desperately then gallop-gallop-gallop! But that finished them, because the back and front legs didn't gallop together, got entangled and down went the horse! The farmer ran up in alarm, thinking that his horse had fallen.

'Take your knee out of my mouth,' mumbled an angry voice, and the farmer stopped suddenly, astounded to hear a human voice coming from the horse. Then he realised what was happening – it was the stage horse with two people in it! Who? It sounded like Julian and Dick. He gave the horse a gentle kick.

'Don't,' said Dick's voice. 'For goodness' sake whoever it is, unzip us! We're suffocating!'

The farmer let out an explosive laugh, bent down and felt for the zip. One good pull and the horse's canvas skin came in half as the zip was undone.

The boys clambered out thankfully.

'Oh – er – thanks very much, Mr Penruthlan,' said Julian, rather embarrassed. 'We – er – we were just having a canter around.'

Mr Penruthlan gave another hearty roar and went off towards the kitchen to finish his meal. Dick and Julian felt very thankful. They carried the legs and head of the horse cautiously towards the barn. They peered in at a window. The Guv'nor was there, striding up and down, looking extremely angry.

Julian waited till he was at the far end of the barn, and then hurriedly pushed the legs and head in the door, as quietly as he could. When the Guv'nor turned around to stride angrily back the first thing he saw was the bundle that was Clopper! He raced over to it at once, and looked out of the door.

But Julian and Dick had gone. They could own

up the next day when things weren't quite so exciting! They slid quietly into the kitchen, feeling hot and untidy, hoping that nobody would notice them.

George and Anne saw them at once. George came over. 'What have you been doing? You've been ages and ages. Do you want any more to eat before everything is finished up?'

'Tell you everything afterwards,' said Julian. 'Yes, we do want something to eat. I've hardly had a thing yet. I'm starving!'

Mr Penruthlan was back in his place eating again. He pointed with his knife at the boys sliding into their seats. 'Ock-ock-oo,' he said, beginning to laugh, and added a few more equally puzzling words.

'Oh, they've been to help you catch the horse that peered in at the window, have they?' said Mrs Penruthlan, nodding. 'Which horse was it?'

'Clopper!' said the farmer, quite clearly, and gave a loud laugh again.

Nobody understood what he meant, so nothing more was said. George and Anne guessed, though, and grinned at the two boys.

It was a wonderful evening, and everyone was

sorry that it had to come to an end. The villagers and the two girls stacked the dirty dishes and plates and the boys carried them to the sink to be washed. The Barnies gave a hand where they could, and the big kitchen was full of chatter and laughter. It was very pleasant indeed.

But at last the kitchen was empty again, and the big lamp turned out. The villagers went home, the Barnies departed. Grandad took Yan's hand and went back to his sheep, saying dolefully that he'd 'et too much and wouldn't be able to sleep a wink, so he wouldn't.'

'Never mind. It was worth it, Grandad,' said Mrs Penruthlan, and shut and locked the kitchen door.

She looked around, tired but happy. There was nothing she liked better than to spend hours upon hours preparing delicious dishes for people and then see them eaten in no time at all! The children thought she was absolutely wonderful.

They were soon all in bed and asleep. The Penruthlans were asleep, too. Only the kitchen cat was awake, watching for mice in the kitchen. She didn't like a crowd. She liked the kitchen to herself!

Next day was fair and warm, although a stiff breeze still blew. Mrs Penruthlan spoke to the four children at breakfast-time.

'I'll be busy today cleaning up the mess. How would you like to take a picnic lunch of some of the remains of the supper and stay out all day? It's a nice day, and you'll enjoy it.'

Nothing could be better! Julian had already planned to make his way to the old tower once used by the Wreckers, and explore it. Now they would have all day to do it in!

'Oh, yes, Mrs Penruthlan, we'd love to do that,' he said. 'We'll get the picnic ready. You've got enough to do!'

But no, Mrs Penruthlan wouldn't let anyone deal with food but herself. She proceeded to pack up enough food for twelve people, or so Julian thought when he saw her preparations!

They set off together happily, with Timmy at their heels. The four farm dogs accompanied them for some way, tearing on in front and then tearing back trying to make Timmy as mad as they were. But Timmy was sedate, walking along as if to say, 'I'm taking these children for a walk, I've no time to play with you. You're only farm dogs!'

'Do we want Yan with us if he turns up?' asked George. 'Do we particularly want him to know what we're doing today?'

Julian considered. 'No, I don't think we *do* want him with us. We may find out something we don't want him to know, or to spread around.'

'Right,' said George. 'Well, just you send him off, then, if he comes. I'm fed up with him.'

Yan did appear, of course. He came up silently on his bare feet. Nobody would have known he was trotting behind if it hadn't been for Timmy. Timmy happily left George's heels and went to say hello to Yan, jumping up at him in delight.

George turned around to see where Timmy was, and saw Yan.

'Julian, there's Yan!' she said.

'Hello, Yan,' said Julian. 'Buzz off today. We're going somewhere alone.'

'I'm coming too,' said Yan, strutting along behind.

'No, you can't come too,' said Julian. 'You buzz off. Off you go.'

Yan's face took on a sulky look. He turned to Anne.

'Can't I come too?' he said, pleadingly.

Anne shook her head.

'No, not today,' she said. 'Another time. Take this sweet, Yan, and go away.'

Yan took the sweet and turned away, his face sulky. He disappeared over the field and was soon lost to sight.

The four children and Timmy went on together, glad of their warm jumpers when the wind blew strongly. Julian gave a sudden groan.

'I'll be glad when we've had our lunch,' he said. 'This bag of food is so heavy it's cutting into my shoulders.'

'Let's wait till we get to the tower and we can put the bags down,' said Dick. 'We'll do a little exploring before we have our lunch. I expect Mrs Penruthlan meant us to stay out to lunch, tea and supper, the amount she's packed for us!'

They hoped they were going in the right direction. They had looked at a map, and found various lanes which they thought would eventually lead to the tower, and had worked out which was the best direction to take.

Julian had his compass and was going by that, leading them down lanes, across fields, along little paths, and sometimes along no paths at all! He felt sure, however, that they were going right. They were making for the coast, anyway.

'Look, there are two hills side by side, or cliffs, are they?' said Anne, pointing. 'I think they're the hills between which we saw that tower.'

'Yes, you're right,' said Dick. 'We're nearly there. I wonder how people got there when the tower and house were lived in. There seems to be no proper road at all.'

They walked on, over a rough field. They soon found themselves in a very narrow, overgrown lane, deep-set between hedges that almost met overhead.

'A green tunnel,' said Anne, pleased. 'Look out for those enormous nettles, Ju.'

At the end of the lane an overgrown path swung sharply right, and there, not far from them, was the tower! They stood and stared at it. This was where the light had flashed a hundred years ago to bring ships to their doom, and where the light had flashed only the other night.

'The tower's falling into ruins,' said Dick. 'Large pieces have dropped out of it. And I expect the house is in ruins, too, although we can't see enough of it at the moment, just a bit of the roof.

Come on. This is going to be fun!'

The tower didn't look the frightening thing it had seemed on the stormy night when the boys saw the flashing light. It just looked a poor old ruin. They made their way to it through high thistles, nettles and willowherb.

'Doesn't *look* as if anyone has been here for years,' said Julian, rather puzzled. 'I wish we'd brought something to cut down these enormous weeds! We can hardly get through them. I'm stung all over with nettles, too.'

They came to the house at last, and a poor, tumbledown ruin it was! The doors had fallen in, the windows were out of shape, and had no glass, the roof was full of holes. An enormous climbing rose rambled everywhere, throwing masses of old-fashioned white roses over walls and roof to hide the ugliness of the ruin.

Only the tower seemed still strong, except at the top, where parts of the wall had crumbled away and fallen. Julian forced his way through the broken doorway into the house. Weeds grew in the floor.

'There's a stone stairway going up the tower!' he called. 'And hey, look here! What's this on each stair?'

'Oil,' said George. 'Someone's been carrying oil up in a can, or a lamp, and has spilt it. Julian, we'd better be careful. That somebody may still be here!'

13 In the Wreckers' tower

Dick and Anne came hurriedly up to the old stone stairway when they heard what Julian and George had said. Oil! That could only mean one thing, a lamp in the tower.

They all stood and looked at the big splashes of oil on each step.

'Come on up,' said Julian at last. 'I'll go first. Be careful how you go because the tower's in a very crumbly state.'

The tower was built at one end of the old house, and its walls were thicker than the house walls. The only entry to it was by a doorway inside the house. In the tower was a stone stairway that went very steeply up in a spiral.

'This must once have been the door of the tower,' said Dick, kicking at a great thick slab of wood that lay mouldering away beside the stone doorway. 'The tower doesn't seem to hold anything but this stone stairway, just a lookout, I suppose.'

'Or a place for signalling to ships to entice them on the rocks,' said George. 'Oh, Timmy, don't push past like that; you nearly made me fall, these stone steps are so steep.'

As Dick said, the tower seemed to hold nothing but a stairway spiralling up steeply. Julian came to the top first and gave a gasp. The view over the sea was astonishing. He could see for miles over the dark cornflower-blue waters. Near the coast the churning of the waves into white breakers and spray showed the hidden rocks that waited for unwary ships.

George came up beside him and stared in wonder, too. What a wonderful sight, blue sky, blue sea, waves pounding over the rocks, and white gulls soaring on the stiff breeze.

Then Dick came up, and Julian gave him a warning. 'Be careful. Don't lean on the walls at all, they're crumbling badly.'

Julian put out his hand and touched the top of the tower wall near him. It crumbled and bits fell away below.

Big pieces had fallen away here and there, leaving great gaps in the wall around the top of the tower. When Anne came up also, Julian took her arm, afraid that with such a crowd up there someone might stumble against a crumbling wall and fall from the tower.

George had hold of Timmy's collar and made him stand still. 'Don't you go putting your great paws up on the wall,' she warned him. 'You'll find yourself down in the nettles below in no time if you do!'

'You can see what a wonderful place this is for flashing a light at night over the sea,' said Dick. 'It could be seen for miles. In the old days, when sailing ships got caught in the storms that rage around this coast at times, they'd be thankful to see a guiding light.'

'But what a light!' said Julian. 'A light that guided them straight on to those great rocks! Let's see now. Are those the rocks near those coves we went to the other day?'

'Yes, I think so,' said Dick. 'But there are rocks and rocks, and coves and coves around here. It's difficult to tell if they're the same ones we saw.'

'The ships that sailed towards the light must have been wrecked on the rocks down there,' said Julian, pointing. 'How did the wreckers get there? There must have been a path from here somewhere.'

'The Wreckers' Way, do you think?' said Dick.

Julian considered. 'I don't know. I guess that the Wreckers' Way must have been a way leading to the sea from inland somewhere, certainly a way that was convenient for the villagers to use. No. I'll tell you what I think happened!'

'What?' said everyone.

'I think, on a stormy night long ago, the people who lived here in this house went up into the tower and flashed their false light to any ship that was sailing out on the waters. Then, in great excitement, they watched it sailing nearer and nearer, perhaps shown up by the lightning, perhaps by the moon.'

Everyone imagined such a ship, and George shivered. Poor wretched ship!

'When the ship reached the rocks and crashed on them, the signallers in the tower gave a different signal, a signal to a watcher up there on the hills,' said Julian, pointing behind him. 'A watcher who was standing on the only spot from which the flash could be seen! Maybe the light gleamed steadily to entice a ship in, but was flashed in code to the watcher on the hills, and the flashing said, 'Ship on rocks. Tell the others, and come to the feast!'

'That's horrible!' said Anne. 'I can't believe it!'

'It *is* difficult to think anyone could be so heartless,' said Julian. 'But I think that's what happened. And then, I think, the people who lived in this house went down from here to the nearby coves and waited for their friends to come along the other way, the Wreckers' Way, wherever that is.'

'It must be a secret way,' said Dick. 'It must have been a way known only to those villagers who *were* Wreckers. After all, wrecking was against the law, and so this whole business of showing lights and wrecking ships must have been kept a dead secret. We heard what Grandad said, that every Wrecker who knew the way had to vow he would tell no one else.'

'Grandad's dad probably lived in this very house, and climbed the stone stairway on a wild night, and lit the lamp that shone out over the stormy sea,' said Julian.

'That's why Yan said he was frightened of this tower,' said George. 'He thinks his grandad's dad still lights it! Well, we know better. Somebody else lights it, somebody who can't be up to any good either!'

'And, don't let's forget, somebody who may still be about somewhere!' said Julian, lowering his voice suddenly.

'Oh! Yes,' said Dick, looking around the little tower as if he expected to see a stranger there, listening. 'I wonder where he keeps his lamp. It's not here.'

'The oil splashes are on almost every one of the stone steps,' said Anne. 'I noticed as I came up. I bet it's a big lamp. It has to give a light far out to sea!'

'Look, it must have been stood on this bit of the wall,' said Dick. 'There are some oily patches here.'

They all looked at the oily patches. Dick bent down and smelt them.

'Yes, paraffin oil,' he said.

George was looking at the wall on the other side of the tower. She called to the other three.

'And here's a patch on *this* side!' she said. 'I know what happened! Once a ship had been caught by the light and was on its way in, the men with the lamp put it on the *other* side of the tower to signal to the watcher on the hills, to tell him the ship was caught!'

'Yes. That's it,' said Anne. 'But who could it be? I'm sure nobody lives *here*, the place is an absolute ruin, open to the wind and the rain. It must be somebody who knows the way here, sees to the light, and does the signalling.'

There was a pause. Dick looked at Julian. The same thought came into their minds. *They* had seen somebody wandering out in the stormy night, twice!

'Could it be Mr Penruthlan, do you think?' said Dick. 'We couldn't *imagine* why he was out here in the storm the first night we came out to watch for the light.'

'No, he's not the man with the light, *he's the watcher on the hills*!' said Julian. 'That's it! That's why he goes out on wild nights, to see if there's a signal from the tower, flashing to say that a ship is coming in!'

There was an even longer pause. Nobody liked that idea at all.

'We know he tells lies, we know he goes through people's pockets, because we saw him,' went on

Julian after a few moments. 'He fits in well. He's the man who goes and stands in that special spot on the hills and watches for a light!'

'What does he do after that?' said Anne. 'Didn't we hear that there were no wrecks here now, because of the lighthouse higher up the coast? What's the point of it all, if there isn't a wreck?'

'Smuggling,' said Julian shortly. 'That's the point. Probably by motorboat. They choose a wild night of storm and wind, when they'll be neither seen nor heard, wait out at sea for the signalling light to show them all's clear, and then come into one of these coves.'

'Yes, and I bet the Wreckers' secret way is used by someone who steals down to the cove and takes the smuggled goods!' said Dick, excited. 'Three or four people, perhaps, if the goods are heavy. Oh! I'm sure we're right.'

'And it's the watcher on the hill who tells his friends, and down they go to the coves together. It's very clever,' Julian said. 'Nobody sees the light on the tower except the boat waiting, and nobody sees the signal inland except the one watcher on the hills. Absolutely foolproof.'

'We're lucky to stumble on it,' said Dick. 'But

what puzzles me is this. I'm pretty certain that the man who lights the lamp didn't come the way *we* came – we'd have seen trodden-down weeds or something. We'd have found some sort of a path his feet had made.'

'Yes. And there wasn't anything, not even a broken thistle,' said Anne. 'There must be some other way into this old house.'

'Of course there is! We've already said there must be a way for the man who lights the lamp to get down to the coves from here!' said George. 'Well, that's the way he gets here, of course. He comes up the passage from the cove. How stupid we are!'

This idea excited them all. Where was the passage? Nobody could imagine! It certainly wasn't in the tower, there was no room for anything in that small tower except for the spiral staircase leading to the top.

'Let's go down,' said Anne, and began to descend the steps. A slight noise below made her stop.

'Go on,' said George, who was just behind her. Anne turned a scared face to her.

'I heard a noise down there,' she whispered.

George turned to Julian immediately. 'Anne thinks there's somebody down there,' she said, in a low voice.

'Come back, Anne,' ordered Julian at once. Anne climbed back, still looking scared.

'Would it be the man who does the lamp?' she whispered. 'Please be careful, Julian. He can't be a nice man!'

'Nice! He must be horrible!' said George, scornfully. 'Are you going down, Ju? Look out, then.'

Julian peered down the stone steps. There was really nothing for it but to go down and see who was there. They couldn't possibly stay up in the tower all day long, hoping that whoever it was would go away!

'What sort of noise did you hear?' Julian asked Anne.

'Well, a sort of scuffling noise,' said Anne. 'It might have been a rat, of course, or a rabbit. It was just a noise, that's all. Something's down there, or somebody!'

'Let's sit down for a moment or two and wait,' said Dick. 'We'll listen hard and see if we can hear anyone.'

So they sat down cautiously, George with her hand on Timmy's collar. They waited and they listened. They heard the wind blowing around the old tower. They heard the distant gulls calling, 'ee-oo, ee-oo, ee-oo'. They heard the thistles rustling their prickles together down below.

But they heard nothing from the kitchen at the foot of the tower. Julian looked at Anne. 'No sound to be heard now,' he said. 'It must have been a rabbit!'

'Perhaps it was,' said Anne, feeling a bit foolish. 'What shall we do then? Go down?'

'Yes. I'll go first though, with Timmy,' said Julian. 'If anyone is lying in wait he'll be annoyed to see Timmy. And Timmy will be even more annoyed to see him!'

Just as Julian was getting up, a noise was distinctly heard from below. It was, as Anne had described, a kind of scuffle, then silence.

'Well, here goes!' said Julian, and began to descend the steps.

The others watched breathlessly. Timmy went with Julian, trying to press past him. He hadn't seemed worried about the noise at all! So perhaps it *was* only a rat or rabbit!

Julian went down slowly. Who was he going to find – an enemy, or a friend? Careful now, Julian, there may be somebody lying in wait!

14 The secret passage

Julian paused on the last step of the spiral staircase and listened. Not a sound came from the nearby room.

'Who's there?' said Julian, sharply. 'I know you're there! I heard you!'

Still not a sound! The kitchen, overgrown with weeds and dark with ivy and the white rambling rose, seemed to be listening to him, but there was no answer!

Julian stepped right into the room and looked around. Nothing was there – nobody was there! The place was absolutely empty and quiet. Julian went through a doorway into another room. That was empty, too. The old house only had four rooms altogether, two of them very tiny, and every one of them was empty. Timmy didn't seem disturbed at all, either, nor did he bark as he certainly would have done if there had been any intruder there.

'Timmy, it's a false alarm,' said Julian, relieved. 'Must have been a rabbit, or even a bit of wall crumbling and falling. What are you sniffing at there?'

Timmy was sniffing with interest at a corner near the doorway. He stood and looked at Julian as if he'd like to tell him something. Julian went over to see what it was.

There was nothing there except for some rather flattened weeds, growing through the floor. Julian couldn't think why Timmy should be interested. However, Timmy soon wandered away and went all around the place, wondering why they had come to such a strange house.

'Come down!' shouted Julian up the stone stairway. 'There doesn't seem to be anyone here, after all. It must have been some small animal that Anne heard.'

The others clattered down in relief.

'I'm sorry I gave you all a shock,' said Anne. 'It did sound like somebody down there! But I'm sure Timmy would have barked if so! He didn't seem at all disturbed.'

'No. I think we can safely say that it was a false alarm,' said Dick. 'What do we do next? Have

our lunch? Or hunt about to see if we can find the
entrance to the passage that leads from here down
to the coves?'

Julian looked at his watch. 'It's not really
time for lunch yet, unless you're all very hungry,'
he said.

'Well, I'm *starting* to feel pretty hungry,'
said Dick. 'But, on the other hand, I feel I can't
wait to find that passage! Where on earth is
the entrance?'

'I've been in all four rooms,' said Julian. 'None
of them seems to have anything but weeds in
them, no old door leading out of the walls, no
trapdoor. It's a puzzle.'

'Well, we'll all have a really good hunt,' said
George. 'This is the sort of thing I like. Timmy,
you hunt, too!'

They began to explore the four rooms of the
old house. As weeds grew more or less all over
the floor they felt that there could be no trapdoor.
If there had been, and the man with the lamp used
it, the weeds would surely have shown signs of it.
But they grew completely undisturbed.

'Listen,' said Julian at last. 'I've got an idea.
We'll make Timmy find the entrance.'

'How?' said George at once.

'Well, we'll make him smell the oil drips on the steps, and follow with his nose any others that have dripped in the weeds,' said Julian. 'I don't suppose the lamp dripped only on the steps. It must have dripped all the way from the passage entrance, wherever it is, to the top of the tower. Couldn't Timmy sniff them out? They'd lead us to the entrance we're trying to find!'

'All right. But I'm starting to think there is no entrance,' said George, getting hold of Timmy's collar. 'We've looked over every single inch of this house. Come on, Tim, you've got to perform a miracle!'

Timmy's nose was firmly placed over the oil drip on the bottom stair.

'Sniff it, Timmy, and follow,' said George.

Timmy knew perfectly well what she meant. George had trained him well! He sniffed hard at the oil and then started up the stone steps for the next oil patch. But George pulled him back.

'No, Tim. Not that way. This way. There must be other oil drips on the floor of the house.'

Timmy amiably turned the other way. He found an oil drip at once, on a patch of weeds growing on the floor. He sniffed it and went on to another and another.

'Good boy, Timmy,' said George, delighted. 'Isn't he clever, Ju? He's following where the man walked when he carried that lamp! Go on, Timmy, where's the next drip?'

It was an easy strong-smelling trail for Timmy to follow! He followed it, sniffing, out of one room into another, smaller one. Then into a third, bigger one, which must have been the main room, for it had a very big fireplace, his nose to the ground. In fact, he went right into the hearth, and there came to a stop. He looked around at George and barked.

'He says the trail ends here,' said George, in excitement. 'So the entrance to the secret passage must be in this big fireplace!'

The others crowded to the hearth. Julian produced his torch and shone it up the chimney. It was an enormous one, although part of the top of it had now fallen away. 'Nothing there,' said Julian. 'But – hey – what's this?'

He now shone his torch to the side of the big fireplace and saw a small, dark cavity there, barely big enough for a man to get into.

'Look!' he said, excited, 'I think we've found it. See that small hole? Well, I bet if we crawl through that we'll find it's the way to the secret passage! Good boy, Timmy!'

'We'll get absolutely *filthy*,' said Anne.

'You *would* say that!' said George, scornfully. 'Who cares? This could be very important, couldn't it, Ju?'

'Definitely!' said Julian. 'If we're on to what we think we are, and that's Smuggling with a capital S, it *is* important. Well, what about it? Lunch first, or exploring that hole?'

'Exploring, of course,' said Dick. 'What about letting Tim go first? I'll give him a leg-up.'

Timmy was hoisted up to the black hole, and disappeared into it with delight. Rabbits? Rats? What were the children after? This was a good game!

'Now I'll go,' said Julian, and clambered up. 'It's a bit difficult to squeeze into.'

He disappeared, and one by one the others also hoisted themselves to the hole and crawled in, too.

The hole was merely an entrance to a narrow standing place at the side of the chimney. Julian got down from the hole, and stood still for a moment, wondering if this was just an old hiding place, and not an entrance to anywhere, after all. But then, just to the right of his feet, he saw another hole that dropped sharply down.

He flashed his torch down, and saw iron hand grips at one side. He called back and told the others. Then he descended into the hole, at first using the grips for his feet and then for his hands as well.

The hole went down as straight as a well. It came to a sudden end, and Julian found himself standing on solid ground. He turned around, flashing his torch.

There was the passage in front of him! It must be the one that led down to the coves, the one that the man with the lamp must have used long ago, when he went to gloat over the groaning ships on the rocks.

Julian could hear the others coming down the shaft. He suddenly thought of Timmy. Where was he? He must have fallen headlong down the hole and found himself suddenly at the bottom. Poor Tim! Julian hoped he hadn't hurt himself, but as he hadn't yelped, perhaps he'd fallen like a cat, on his feet!

He called up to the others. 'I've found the passage. It starts at the bottom of the shaft. I'll go along it a little way and wait for you all to come. Then we can keep together in a line.'

Soon everyone was safely down the shaft. George began to worry about Timmy. 'He *must* have hurt himself, Ju! Falling all that way; oh, dear, where is he?'

'We'll soon come across him, I expect,' said Julian. 'Now, keep close together, everybody. The path goes downwards pretty steeply, as you might expect.'

It certainly did. In places the four children almost slithered along. Then Julian discovered iron staples fixed here and there in the steepest places, and after that they held on to them in the most slippery spots.

'These iron staples would be really useful to anyone coming *up*,' said Julian. 'It'd be almost impossible to climb up this passage without something to help the climber to pull himself up. Ah, here's a more level stretch.'

The level part soon became much wider. And then suddenly it became a cave! The four came out into it in surprise. It was low-roofed, and the walls were made of black rock that glistened in the light of the torch.

'I wish I could find Timmy,' said George, uneasily. 'I can't even hear him anywhere!'

'We'll go on till we come to the cove,' said Julian. 'This must lead us right down to the shore, probably to the very cove where the ships were wrecked. Look, there's a kind of rocky arch leading out of this cave.'

They went through the archway and into yet another passage that wound between jutting rocks, which made it a bit difficult to get through at times. Then suddenly the passage divided into two. One fork went meandering off towards the seaward side, the other into the cliff.

'Better take the seaward side,' said Julian. They were just going to take the right-hand passage when George stopped and clutched at Julian. 'Listen!' she said. 'I can hear Timmy!'

They all stopped and listened. George had the sharpest ears of the lot, and she could hear him barking. So could the others after a few moments. Bark-bark-bark! Bark-bark-bark! Yes, it was Timmy all right!

'Timmy!' yelled George, making the others jump almost out of their skins. 'TIMMY!'

'He can't hear you all this way away,' said Dick. 'You made me jump. Come on, we'll have to take the cliff passage. Timmy's barking comes from that direction, not this.'

'Yes, I agree,' said Julian. 'We'll go and collect him, and then come back and take the other passage. I'm sure it leads down to the sea.'

They made their way along the left-hand passage. It wasn't difficult, because it was much wider than the one they had already come down. Timmy's barking became louder and louder as they went down. George whistled piercingly, hoping that Timmy would come rushing up. But he didn't.

'It's funny that he doesn't come,' said George, worried. 'I think he must be hurt. TIMMY!'

The passage wound around a corner, and then once more divided into two. To the children's surprise they saw a rough door set into the rocky wall of the passage on the left-hand side. A door! How very extraordinary!

'Look, a door!' said Dick, amazed. 'And a really strong one, too.'

'Timmy's behind it!' said George. 'He must have gone through it and it shut behind him. Timmy! We're here! We're coming!'

She pushed at the door, but it didn't open. She saw that it was lightly latched, and lifted the old iron latch. The door opened easily and all four went through into a strange cave beyond. It was more like a low-roofed room!

Timmy flung himself at them as soon as they came through the door. He wasn't hurt. He was so pleased to see them that he barked the place down! 'Woof! WOOOOOF!'

'Oh, Timmy, how did you get here?' said George, hugging him. 'Did the door click behind you? What a strange place this is! It's a storeroom – look at all the boxes and crates and things!'

They looked around the strange cave, and at that moment there was a soft click. Then something slid smoothly into place. Julian leapt to the door and tried to open it.

'It's locked! Somebody's locked it, and bolted it! I heard them. Let us out, let us out!'

15 Locked in the cave

Dick, George and Anne looked at one another in
dismay. Someone must have been lying in wait for
them. Someone must have captured Timmy and
shut him up. And now they were captured, too!

Timmy began to bark when Julian shouted. He
ran to the door. Julian was hammering on it and
even kicking it.

A voice came from the other side of the door, a
drawling voice, sounding rather amused.

'You came at an awkward time, that's all, and
you must remain where you are till tomorrow.'

'Who are you?' said Julian fiercely. 'How dare
you lock us in like this!'

'I believe you have food and drink with you,'
said the voice. 'I noticed the packs on your backs,
which I presume contain food. That's lucky for
you! Now be sensible. You must pay the penalty
for being inquisitive!'

'You let us out!' shouted Julian, enraged at the

cool voice with its impertinent tone.

He kicked the door again out of temper, although he knew that it wasn't the slightest use!

There was no reply. Whoever it was outside the cave door had gone. Julian gave the door one last furious kick and looked around at the others.

'That man must have been watching us from somewhere. Probably followed us all the way to the old house, and saw the packs on our backs then. It must have been him that you heard down in the house when we were in the tower, Anne.'

Timmy barked again. He was still at the door. George called him. 'Tim! It's no use! The door's locked. Oh dear, why did we let you go into that hole first? If you hadn't run on ahead and somehow got yourself caught, you'd have been able to protect us when those men lay in wait!'

'Well, what do we do now?' said Anne, trying to sound brave.

'What *can* we do?' said George. 'Nothing at all! Here we are, locked and bolted in a cave inside the cliff, with nobody near except the man who locked us in. If anybody's got any ideas I'd like to hear them!'

'You sound so cross!' said Anne. 'I suppose

there isn't anything to do but wait till we're let out. I only hope that man remembers we're here. Nobody else knows where we are.'

'Horrible thought!' said Dick. 'Still, I expect that Mrs Penruthlan would raise the alarm, and a search party would set out to find us.'

'Some hope they'd have!' said George. 'Even if they did trace us to the old tower, they wouldn't know the secret entrance to the passage!'

'Let's look on the bright side,' said Julian, undoing the pack from his back. 'Let's have some food.'

Everybody cheered up at once. 'I'm really hungry,' said Anne in surprise. 'It must be past our lunch-time now. Well, anyway, eating will be something to do!'

They had a very good meal and felt thankful that Mrs Penruthlan had packed up so much food. If they weren't going to be let out till the next day they would need plenty to eat!

They examined the boxes and crates. Some were very old. All were empty. There was a big seaman's chest there, too, with 'Abram Trelawny' painted on it. They lifted the lid. That was empty too, save for one old brass button.

'Abram Trelawny,' said Dick, looking at the name. 'He must have been a sailor on one of the ships that the Wreckers enticed to the rocks. This chest must have been rolled up on the beach by the waves and brought up here. I expect this cave was the place where the man who owned that old house took his share of the booty and hid it.'

'Yes, I think you're right,' said Julian. 'That's why it has a door that can be locked. The Wreckers probably stored a lot of valuable things here from different wrecks, and didn't want any other Wrecker to creep up from the cave and take them. What a horrible lot they must have been! Well, there doesn't seem anything of real interest here.'

It was very, very boring in the cave. The children used only one torch because they were afraid that if they used the others they had brought they might exhaust all the batteries, and then have to be in the dark.

Julian examined the cave from top to bottom to see if there was any possible way of escape. But there wasn't. That was obvious. The cave walls were made of solid rocks, and there wasn't a hole anywhere through which to escape, big or small!

'That man said we'd come at an awkward

time,' said Julian, throwing himself down on the ground. 'Why? Are they expecting some smuggled goods tonight? They've signalled out to sea twice already this week, as *we* know. Hasn't the boat they expected come along yet? If so, they must be expecting it tonight, and so we've come at an awkward time!'

'If only we weren't locked in this horrible cave!' said George. 'We could have spied on them and seen what they were up to, and might even have been able to stop them somehow, or get word to the police.'

'Well, we can't now,' said Dick gloomily. 'Timmy, you were an idiot to get caught; you really were.'

Timmy put his tail down and looked as gloomy as Dick. He didn't like being in this low-roofed cave. Why didn't they open the door and go out? He went to the door and whined, scraping at it with his feet.

'No good, Tim. It won't open,' said Anne. 'I think he's thirsty, George.'

There was nothing for Timmy to drink except home-made lemonade, and he didn't seem to like that very much.

'Don't waste it on him if he doesn't like it,' said Julian, hastily. 'We may be glad of it ourselves tomorrow.'

Dick glanced at his watch. 'Only half past two!' he groaned. 'Hours and hours to wait. Let's have a game of some sort, noughts and crosses would be better than nothing.'

They played noughts and crosses till they were sick of them. They played word games and guessing games. They had a light tea at five o'clock and began to wonder what Mrs Penruthlan would think when they didn't turn up that evening.

'If Mr Penruthlan is mixed up in this, and it's pretty certain that he is,' said Julian, 'he'll not be best pleased to be told to fetch the police to look for *us*! It's just the one night he won't want the police about!'

'I think you're wrong,' said George. 'I think he'd be delighted to have the police looking for lost children, and not poking their noses into *his* business tonight!'

'I hadn't thought of that,' said Julian.

How slowly the time went by. They yawned, talked, fell silent, argued and played with

Timmy. Julian's torch flickered out and they took Dick's instead.

'Good thing we brought more than one torch!' said Anne.

Half past nine came and they all began to feel sleepy.

'Let's try to go to sleep,' said Dick, yawning hugely. 'There's a sandy spot over there, softer to lie on than this rock. What about trying to sleep?'

They all thought it was a good idea and went to the sandy spot. It was better than the hard rock. They wriggled about in the sand and made dents for their bodies to lie in.

'It's still hard,' complained George. 'Oh, Timmy, *don't* snuffle all around my face. Lie down beside me and Anne and go to sleep, too!'

Timmy lay down on George's legs. He put his nose on his paws and heaved a huge sigh.

'I hope Timmy's not going to do *that* all night,' said Anne. 'What a draught!'

Although they thought they couldn't possibly go to sleep, they did. Timmy did, too, although he kept one ear open and one eye ready to open. He was on guard! No one could open that door or even come near it without Timmy hearing!

At about eleven o'clock Timmy opened one eye and pricked up both ears. He listened, not taking his head off George's legs. He opened the other eye.

Then he sat up and listened harder. George woke up when he moved and stretched out a hand to Timmy.

'Tim, lie down,' she whispered. But Timmy didn't. He gave a small whine.

George sat up, fully awake. Why was Timmy whining? Was there something going on outside the door, men passing perhaps, on their way to the cove? Had the light been flashing out to sea and had it brought in the boat the men were waiting for?

She put her hand on Timmy's collar. 'What is it?' she whispered, expecting Timmy to growl when he next heard something. But he didn't growl. He whined again.

Then he shook off George's hand and went to the door. George switched on her torch, puzzled. Timmy scraped at the door and whined again. But he still didn't growl.

'Ju! I think someone's at the door!' called George, suddenly, in a low voice. 'I think Timmy can hear a search party or something. Wake up!'

Everyone awoke suddenly. George repeated her words again.

'Timmy's not growling. That means it's not our enemies he hears,' she added. 'He'd growl like anything at the man who locked us in.'

'Be quiet for a moment and listen,' said Julian. 'Let's see if we can hear anything ourselves. We haven't got Timmy's sharp ears, but we might be able to hear *some*thing.'

They sat absolutely still, listening. Then Julian nudged Dick. He'd heard something.

'Quiet!' he breathed. They listened again, hardly breathing.

They heard a little scrabbling noise at the door. Then it stopped. George expected Timmy to break out into a fusillade of barks at once, but he didn't. He stood there with his head on one side and his ears pricked. He gave an excited little whine and suddenly scraped at the door again.

Somebody whispered outside the door, and Timmy whined and ran to George and then back to the door again. Everyone was puzzled.

Julian got up and went to the door himself, his feet making no sound. Yes, there was definitely somebody outside, two people, perhaps, whispering to one another.

'Who's there?' said Julian suddenly. 'I can hear you outside. Who is it?'

There was dead silence for a moment, and then a small familiar voice answered softly:

'It's me. Yan.'

'Yan! Is it really you?'

'Yes.'

There was an amazed silence in the cave. Yan! Yan at this time of night outside the door of the very cave they were locked in! Were they dreaming?

Timmy went mad when he heard Yan speaking to Julian. He flung himself at the door, barking and yelping. Julian put his hand on his collar. 'Be quiet, Tim! You'll spoil everything! Be *quiet*!'

Timmy stopped. Julian spoke to Yan again. 'Yan, have you got a light?'

'No, no light. It's dark here,' said Yan. 'Can I come to you?'

'Yes, of course. Listen, Yan. Do you know how to unlock and unbolt a door?' asked Julian.

'Yes,' said Yan. 'Are you locked in?'

'Yes,' said Julian. 'But the key may be in the

lock. Feel and see. Feel for the bolts, too. Slide them back and turn the key if there is one.'

The four in the cave held their breath as they heard Yan's hands wandering over the stout door in the dark, tapping here and there to find the bolts and the lock.

Then they heard the bolts being slid smoothly back. How they hoped their captor had left the key in the lock!

'Here's a key,' said Yan's voice suddenly. 'But it's so stiff. My hand isn't strong enough to turn it.'

'Try both hands at once,' said Julian urgently.

They heard Yan trying, panting with his efforts. But the key wouldn't turn.

'Oh no!' said Dick. 'So near and yet so far!'

Anne pushed Dick out of the way, an idea suddenly flooding into her mind. 'Yan! Listen to me, Yan. Take the key out of the lock and push it under the bottom of the door. Do you hear me?'

'Yes, I heard,' said Yan, and they heard him tugging at the key.

There was a sharp noise as it came suddenly out of the lock. Then it appeared under the bottom of the door, slid through carefully by Yan!

Julian snatched it up and put it into the lock on his side. He turned the key, and unlocked the door. What wonderful luck!

16 Wreckers' Way

Julian flung open the door. Timmy leapt past him and yelped with delight to find Yan standing outside. He fawned on the boy and licked him, and Yan laughed.

'Let's get out of here, quick!' said Dick. 'That man may come back at any moment, you never know.'

'Right. Explanations later,' said Julian.

He hustled everyone out, took the key from the inside lock and shut the door. He inserted the key into the outside lock and turned it. He shot the bolts, took out the key and put it into his pocket. He grinned at Dick.

'Now if that man comes along to see how we are he won't even know we're gone! He won't be able to get in to see if we're there or not.'

'Where shall we go now?' asked Anne, feeling as if she was in a strange kind of dream.

Julian stood and considered. 'It'd be madness

to go back up the passage and into the old house,' he said. 'If there's any signalling going on, and there's pretty certain to be, we'll be caught again. We'd be sure to make a noise scrambling out of that hole in the fireplace.'

'Well, let's take that other passage we saw, the right-hand one,' said George. 'Look, there it is.' She shone her torch on it. 'Where does it lead to, Yan?'

'To the beach,' said Yan. 'I went down it when I was looking for you all, but you weren't there, so I came back and found that door. There's nobody on the beach.'

'Well, let's go down there, then,' said Dick. 'Once we're out of danger's way we can plan what's best to do.'

They went along the other passage, their torch showing them the way. It was a steep tunnel, and they found it hard going. Anne managed to give Yan a squeeze.

'You were clever to find us!' she said, and Yan gave her a smile, which she couldn't see because of the dark.

They heard the sound of waves at last and came out into the open air. It was a windy night but stars were shining in the sky, and gave a good light after the darkness of the passage.

'Where are we exactly?' said Dick, looking around.

Then he saw they were on the same beach as they had been a few days before, but a good way farther along.

'Can we get back to the farm from here?' said Julian, stopping to work out exactly where they were. 'Hey! I think we'd better hurry. The tide's coming in! We'll be cut off if we don't look out!'

A wave ran up the sand almost to their feet. Julian took a quick look at the cliff behind them. It was very steep. They certainly couldn't climb it in the darkness! Would there be time to look for a cave to sit in till the tide went out again?

Another wave ran up, and Julian's feet felt suddenly wet.

'Oh no!' he said. 'This is getting serious. The next big one will sweep us off our feet. I wish the moon was out. These stars give such a faint light.'

'Yan, is there a cave we can go to, a cave open to the air, not inside the cliff?' said George, anxiously.

'I'll take you back by the Wreckers' Way,' said Yan, surprisingly. 'Come with me.'

'Of course, you said you knew the Wreckers' Way,' said Julian, remembering. 'If it comes out near here, we're in luck! Lead on, Yan. You're amazing! But hurry, our feet got wet again just then, and at any moment a giant of a wave may come!'

Yan took the lead. He led them into cove after cove, and then came to a larger one than usual. He took them to the back of the cove, and led them a little way up a cliff-path.

He came to a great rock. He squeezed behind it and the others followed one by one. Nobody could ever have guessed that there was a way into the cliff behind that rock.

'Now we're in the Wreckers' Way,' said Yan proudly, and led them on again.

But suddenly he stopped and the others all bumped into one another. Timmy gave a short, warning bark, and George put her hand on his collar.

'Somebody's coming!' whispered Yan, and pushed them back.

Sure enough, they could hear voices in the

distance. They turned and hurried back. They didn't want to walk into any more trouble!

Yan got to the front and led them back to the big rock. He was trembling. They all squeezed out behind it, and Yan went along the cliff face to a tiny cave, really only a big ledge with an overhanging roof.

'Sssssssss!' he said warningly, sounding like a snake!

They sat down and waited. Two men came out from behind the rock, one a big man, and one a small one. Nobody could see them clearly, but Julian hissed into Dick's ear: 'I'm sure that's Mr Penruthlan! See how enormous he is!'

Dick nodded. It was no surprise to him to think that the giant farmer should be mixed up in this. The five children held their breath and watched.

Yan nudged Dick and pointed out to sea.

'Boat coming!' he whispered.

Dick could see and hear nothing. But in a few moments he did hear something, the whirr of a fast motorboat! What sharp ears Yan must have! The others heard the noise, too, through the crashing of the waves on the rocks.

'No light,' whispered Yan, as the noise of the

boat grew louder.

'He'll be on the rocks!' said Dick. But before the boat got to the rocks, the engine stopped. The children could just make out the boat now, swaying up and down beyond the barrier of rocks. Evidently it wasn't going to try and come any farther in.

Now the watchers could hear voices again. The two men who had come down Wreckers' Way were standing below the big rock that hid the entrance, talking. One leapt down to a rock farther down, and disappeared. The other man was left standing alone.

'It was the big man who leapt down,' whispered Julian. 'Where's he gone? Ah, there he is! You can just see him moving behind that rock down there. What's he got?'

'A boat!' whispered Yan. 'He has a boat down there, pulled up high out of reach of the big waves. There's a pool there. He's going to row out to the other boat.'

The children strained their eyes to watch. The sky was clear, but the only light they had was from the stars, and it was difficult to see anything more than moving shadows or outlines.

Then there came the sound of oars in rowlocks, and a moving black shadow of a rowing boat and man could be seen faintly, going over the waves.

'Does he know the way through that mass of rocks?' wondered Dick. 'He must know this coast well to risk rowing out through the rocks at high tide in the dead of night!'

'Why is he doing it?'

'He's getting smuggled goods from the motorboat,' said Julian. 'Who knows what! There, I've lost him in the darkness.'

So had everyone. They could no longer hear the oars either, for the crashing of the waves on the rocks drowned every other sound.

Beyond the rocks lay the motorboat, but only Yan's sharp eyes could see it even faintly in the starlight. Once, in a sudden silence of the waves, there came the exchange of voices over the water.

'He's reached the motorboat,' said Dick. 'He'll be back in a minute.'

'Look! The second man is going down to the cove now, going to help the first one in, I expect,' said Julian. 'What about us escaping through the Wreckers' Way while we've got the chance?'

'Good idea,' said George, scrambling up. 'Come on, Timmy! Home!'

They went to the great rock and squeezed behind it once more into the entrance of the Wreckers' Way. Then, Yan once more leading, they went up the secret passage, flicking on the torch very thankfully.

'Where does the Wreckers' Way come out?' asked Anne.

'In a shed at Tremannon Farm,' said Yan, to the astonishment of everyone.

'So it's very nice and handy for Mr Penruthlan!' said George. 'I wonder how many times he's been up on the hills at night, and has been warned by the tower light to go down Wreckers' Way to the cove and collect smuggled goods from some boat or other! A very good plan, and impossible for anyone to find out.'

'Except us!' said Dick in a pleased voice. 'We got on to it pretty well. There's not much we don't know about Mr Penruthlan now!'

They went on and on. The passage was fairly straight and had probably been the bed of an underground stream at some time. The way was smooth to the feet.

'We've walked about a mile, I expect!' groaned Dick, at last. 'How far now, Yan? Will we soon be back?'

'Yes,' said Yan.

Anne suddenly remembered that nobody knew how it was that Yan had found them that night. She turned to him.

'Yan, how did you find us tonight? It seemed like a miracle when we woke up to find you outside that locked door!'

'It was easy,' said Yan. 'You said to me: "Go away. Don't come with us today." So I went back a little way. But I followed you. I followed you to the old house, although I was frightened.'

'I bet you were!' said Dick with a grin. 'Well, go on.'

'I hid,' said Yan. 'You went up into the tower a long time. I came out into the room below, and—'

'It was *you* we heard scuffling there, then!' said Anne. 'We wondered who it was!'

'Yes,' said Yan. 'I sat down on some weeds in a corner, and waited till you came down, and then I hid again, but I watched you through a hole from outside. I saw you go through the fireplace.

One minute you were there. The next you were gone. I was frightened.'

'So it was you who flattened down that patch of weeds that Timmy sniffed at?' said Dick. 'Well, what did you do next?'

'I was going to come too,' said Yan. 'But the hole was so dark and black. I stood in the fireplace for a long time, hoping you'd come back.'

'Then what happened?' said Dick.

'Then I heard voices,' said Yan. 'I thought it was you all coming back. But it wasn't. It was men. So I ran away and hid in the nettles.'

'What a place to choose!' said George.

'Then I was hungry,' said Yan, 'and I went back to Grandad's hut for food. He was angry with me for leaving him, and he made me work for him all day.'

'So you've been on the hills all day, knowing we were down in that passage!' said Julian. 'Didn't you say anything to anyone?'

'I went down to Tremannon Farm to see if you were back when it grew dark,' said Yan. 'But you weren't there. Only the Barnies were there, giving another show. I didn't see Mr or Mrs Penruthlan. I knew then that you must still be down in that dark hole. I was afraid the men had hurt you.'

'So you came all the way again in the dark!' said Julian, astonished. 'You're brave!'

'I was very frightened,' said Yan. 'My legs shook at the knees like my grandad's. I climbed in at the hole, and at last I found you.'

'With no torch to light the way!' said Dick, and clapped the small boy on the back. 'You're a real friend, Yan! Timmy knew you all right when you came to the locked door. He didn't even bark! He knew it was you.'

'I wanted to save Timmy too,' said Yan. 'Timmy's my friend.'

George said nothing to that. She was thinking rather unwillingly that Yan was an amazingly brave young man, and that she had been silly and unkind to resent Timmy's liking for him. What a good thing he *had* liked Timmy!

Yan suddenly stopped.

'We're there,' he said. 'We're at Tremannon Farm. Look above your heads.'

Julian flashed his torch upwards, and stared. An open trapdoor was just above them.

'The trapdoor's open!' he said. 'Someone came down here tonight!'

'And we know who!' said Dick, grimly. 'Mr Penruthlan and his friend! Where does that trapdoor lead to, Yan?'

'Into a corner of the machine shed,' said Yan. 'When the trapdoor's shut, it's covered with sacks of corn or onions. They've been moved to open the way down.'

They all climbed out. Julian flashed the torch around the shed. Yes, there were the machines and the tools. Who would have thought that the sacks he'd seen in here the other day were hiding the trapdoor that led to the Wreckers' Way!

17 *Long after midnight!*

A rat suddenly shot out from a corner of the shed, and tore across to the open trapdoor. Timmy gave a bark and leapt after it. He just stopped himself from taking a header through the trapdoor by sliding along on all four feet and coming to a stop at the entrance.

He stood up and looked down the hole, his head tilted to one side.

'Look, he's listening,' said Anne. 'Is there someone coming, those men, perhaps, with the smuggled goods?'

'No, he's only listening for the rat,' said Julian. 'I tell you what we'll do! We'll shut the trapdoor and pile sacks and boxes and everything on top of it! Then when the men come up, they'll find themselves trapped. They won't be able to get out. If we can get the police in time, they'll be able to catch them easily.'

'Good idea!' said Dick. 'Brilliant! How angry

those two men will be when they come to the trapdoor and find it shut! They can't get out the other way because the tide's up.'

'I'd like to see Mr Penruthlan's face when he sees the trapdoor shut, and feels a whole lot of things piled on top of it!' said Julian. 'He'll make a few more of his strange noises!'

'Ooh – ah – ock,' said Dick, solemnly. 'Come on, help me with the trapdoor, Ju, it's heavy.'

They shut the big trapdoor and then began to drag sacks, boxes and even some kind of heavy farm machine on top of the trapdoor. Now certainly nobody could open it from underneath.

They were hot and very dirty by the time they had finished. They were also beginning to feel very tired.

'Phew!' said Dick. 'I'm glad that's done. Now we'd better go to the farmhouse and show ourselves to Mrs Penruthlan.'

'Oh dear, do we tell her about her husband, and how he's mixed up in this horrible smuggling?' said Anne. 'I really like her. I expect she's very worried about us, too.'

'Yes. It's going to be a bit difficult,' said Julian, sadly. 'Better let me do most of the talking. Come on, we'll go. Don't make too much row or we'll set the dogs barking. I'm surprised they haven't yelled their heads off already!'

It was a bit surprising. Usually the farm dogs barked the place down if there was any unusual noise in the night. The five children and Timmy left the machine shed and made their way towards the farmhouse. George pulled at Julian's arm.

'Look,' she said, in a low voice. 'See those lights up in the hills? What are they?'

Julian looked. He could see moving lights here and there up on the hills. He was puzzled. Then he made a guess.

'I bet Mrs Penruthlan has sent out searchers for us,' he said, 'and they've got torches. They're hunting for us on the hills. I hope all the Barnies aren't out after us too.'

They came to the farmyard, moving very quietly. The big barn, used by the Barnies for their show, was in darkness. Julian pictured it full of benches, left from that night's show. The memory of Mr Penruthlan turning out the pockets of the clothes left and hunting through the drawers in the chest used by the Barnies, came into his mind.

A sharp whisper made them stop very suddenly. George put her hand on Timmy's collar to stop him growling or barking. Who was this now?

None of the little company answered or moved. The whisper came again.

'Here! I'm here!'

Still nobody moved. They were all puzzled. Who was waiting there in the shadows, and for whom was he waiting? The whisper came again, a little louder.

'Here! Over here!'

And then, as if too impatient to wait any longer, the whisperer moved out into the yard. Julian couldn't see who it was in the dark, and he quickly flashed his torch on the man.

It was the Guv'nor, grim-faced as ever! He flinched as the light fell on his face, took a few steps back and disappeared around a corner. Timmy growled.

'Well! How many *more* people wander about at night here?' said Dick. 'That was the Guv'nor. What was *he* doing?'

'I give up,' said Julian. 'I'm getting too tired to think straight. I wouldn't be surprised to see Clopper the horse peering around a corner at us, and saying "Peepo!"'

Everyone chuckled. It was just the kind of thing Clopper *would* do if he were really alive!

They came to the farmhouse. It was full of light, upstairs and downstairs. The curtains weren't drawn across the kitchen window and the children looked in as they passed. Mrs Penruthlan was sitting there, her hands clasped, looking extremely worried.

They opened the kitchen door and trooped in. Yan too. Mrs Penruthlan leapt up at once and ran to them. She hugged Anne, she tried to hug George, she said all kinds of things at top speed, and to the children's dismay they saw that she was crying.

'Oh, where *have* you been?' she said, tears pouring down her face. 'The men are out looking for you, and all the dogs, and the Barnies too. They've been looking for ages! And Mr Penruthlan's not home, either. I don't know where *he* is, he's gone too! Oh, what a terrible evening. But thank goodness you're safe!'

Julian saw that she was badly upset. He took her arm gently and led her to a chair.

'Don't worry,' he said. 'We're all safe. We're

sorry you've been upset.'

'But where have you *been*?' wept Mrs Penruthlan. 'I pictured you drowned, or lost on the hills, or fallen into quarries. And where's Mr Penruthlan? He went out at seven and there's been not a sign of him since!'

The children felt uncomfortable. They thought they knew where Mr Penruthlan was, getting smuggled goods from the motorboat, and carrying them back with his friend, up the Wreckers' Way!

'Now just you tell me what you've been doing,' said Mrs Penruthlan, drying her eyes, and sounding unexpectedly determined. 'Upsetting everybody like this!'

'Well,' said Julian, 'it's a long story, but I'll try to make it short. Strange things have been happening, Mrs Penruthlan.'

He plunged into the whole story, the old tower, Grandad's tale of the flashing light, their journey to explore the tower, the secret passage to the Wreckers' cove, their imprisonment and escape, and then Julian stopped.

How was he to tell poor Mrs Penruthlan that one of the smugglers was her husband? He glanced at the others desperately. Anne began to cry, and George felt very much like it, too. It was Yan who suddenly spoke and broke the news.

'We saw Mr Penruthlan in the cove,' he said, glad of a chance to put in a word. 'We saw him!'

Mrs Penruthlan stared at Yan, and then at the embarrassed, anxious faces of the other children.

'You saw him in the cove?' she said. 'You didn't! What was he doing there?'

'We think, we think he must be one of the smugglers,' said Julian, awkwardly. 'We think we saw him get into a boat and row to the motorboat beyond the rocks. If so, he – well – he may get into trouble, Mrs Penr—'

He didn't finish, because, to his enormous surprise, Mrs Penruthlan jumped up from her chair in a rage.

'You wicked boy!' panted Mrs Penruthlan, sounding suddenly out of breath. 'You bad, wicked boy, saying things like that about Mr Penruthlan, who's the straightest, honestest, most honourable man who ever lived! Him a smuggler! Him in with those wicked men! I'll box your ears till you eat your words and serve you right!'

Julian was amazed at the change in the cheerful

farmer's wife. Her face was red, her eyes were blazing, and somehow she seemed to be taller. He had never seen anyone so angry in his life! Yan went promptly under the table.

Timmy growled. He liked Mrs Penruthlan, but he felt he really couldn't allow her to set about his friends. She faced Julian, trembling with anger.

'Now you apologise!' she said. 'Or I'll give you such a telling off as you've never had in your life before. And you just wait and see what Mr Penruthlan will say when he comes back and hears the things you've said about him!'

What a tiger she was! Julian put his hand on her arm.

'Don't get so upset,' he said. 'I'm very sorry to have made you so angry.'

Mrs Penruthlan shook his hand off her arm.

'Angry! I should think I *am* angry!' she said. 'To think anyone should say those things about Mr Penruthlan. That wasn't him down in Wreckers' Cove. I know it wasn't. I only wish I knew *where* he was! I'm that worried!'

'He's down Wreckers' Way,' announced Yan from his safe vantage point under the table. 'We put the trapdoor down over him.'

'Down Wreckers' Way!' cried Mrs Penruthlan and to the children's great relief she sank down into a chair again. She turned to Julian, questioningly.

He nodded. 'Yes. We came up that way from the beach – Yan knew it. It comes up in a corner of the machine shed, through a trapdoor. We – er – we shut the trapdoor and piled sacks and things on it. I'm afraid, well, I'm afraid Mr Penruthlan can't get out!'

Mrs Penruthlan's eyes almost dropped out of her head. She opened and shut her mouth several times, rather like a goldfish gasping for breath. All the children felt very uncomfortable and extremely sorry for her.

'I don't believe it,' she said at last. 'It's a bad dream. It's not real. Mr Penruthlan will come walking in here at any moment, at any moment, I tell you! He's not down in the Wreckers' Way. He's not a bad man. He'll come walking in, you just see!'

There was silence after this, and in the silence a sound could be heard. The sound of big boots walking over the farmyard. Clomp-clomp-clomp-clomp!

'I'm frightened!' squealed Yan, suddenly, and made everyone jump.

The footsteps came around the kitchen wall, and up to the kitchen door.

'I know who that is!' said Mrs Penruthlan, jumping up. 'I know who that is.'

The door opened and somebody walked in. Mr Penruthlan!

His wife ran to him and flung her arms around him. 'You've come walking in! I said you would. Thank goodness you've come!'

Mr Penruthlan looked tired, and the children, silent with amazement at seeing him, saw that he was wet through. He looked around at them in great surprise.

'What are these children up for?' he said, and they all gaped in surprise.

He was talking properly! His words were quite clear, except that he lisped over his s's.

'Oh, Mr Penruthlan, the tales these bad children have told about you!' cried his wife. 'They said you were a smuggler. They said they'd seen you in Wreckers' Cove going out to a motorboat to get smuggled goods, they said you were trapped in Wreckers' Way, they'd put the trapdoor down, and—'

Mr Penruthlan pushed his wife away from him and swung around on the astounded children. They were very alarmed. How had he escaped from Wreckers' Way? Surely even his great strength couldn't lift up all the things they had piled on top of the trapdoor? How fierce this giant of a man looked, with his mane of black hair, his shaggy eyebrows drawn over his deep-set eyes, and his dense black beard!

'What's all this?' he demanded, and they gaped again at his speech.

They were so used to his strange noises that it seemed amazing he could speak properly after all.

'Well,' began Julian, awkwardly, 'we – er – we've been exploring that tower – and – er – finding out a bit about the smugglers, and we *really* thought we recognised you in Wreckers' Cove, and we thought we'd trapped you, and your friend, by shutting the trapdoor and—'

'This is important,' said Mr Penruthlan, and his voice sounded urgent. 'Forget all this about thinking I'm a smuggler. You've got things wrong. I'm working with the police. It was someone else down in the cove, not me. I've been on the coast, it's true, watching out, and getting drenched, as you can see, all to no purpose. What do you know? What's this about the trapdoor? Did you really close it, and trap those men?'

All this was so completely astonishing that for a moment nobody could say a word. Then Julian leapt up.

'Yes, sir! We did put the trapdoor down, and if you want to catch those men, send for the police, and we'll do it! We've only got to wait beside the trapdoor till the smugglers come!'

'Right,' said Mr Penruthlan. 'Come along. Hurry!'

18 Dick gets an idea!

In the greatest surprise and excitement the five children rushed to the kitchen door to follow Mr Penruthlan. Yan had scrambled out from beneath the table, determined not to miss anything. But at the door the farmer turned around.

'Not all of you,' he said.

'I'll keep the girls here with me,' said Mrs Penruthlan, who had forgotten her dismay and anger completely in this new excitement. 'Yan, come here.'

But Yan had slipped out with the others. Nothing in the world would make him miss this new excitement! Timmy had gone too, of course, as excited as the rest.

'What goings-on in the early hours of the morning!' said Mrs Penruthlan, sitting down suddenly again. 'To think that Mr Penruthlan never told me he was working to find those smugglers! We knew it was going on, around this coast, and to think he was keeping a watch, and never told me!'

Julian and Dick had completely forgotten that they felt tired. They hurried over the farmyard with Mr Penruthlan, Yan a little way behind, and Timmy leaping around like a mad thing. They came to the machine shed and went in.

'We piled—' began Julian, and then suddenly stopped. Mr Penruthlan's powerful torch was shining on the corner where the trapdoor was fixed.

It was open! Unbelievably open! The sacks and boxes that the children had dragged over it were now scattered to one side.

'Look at that!' said Julian, amazed. 'Who's opened it? The smugglers have got out, with their smuggled goods, and they've gone. We're beaten!'

Mr Penruthlan made a very angry noise, and flung the trapdoor shut with a resounding bang. He was about to say something more when there came the sound of voices not far off. It was the Barnies returning from their search for the children.

They saw the light in the shed and peered in.

When they saw Julian and Dick they cried out in delight. 'Where were you? We've searched everywhere for you!'

Julian and Dick were so disappointed at finding their high hopes dashed that they could hardly respond to the Barnies' delighted greetings. They felt suddenly very tired again, and Mr Penruthlan seemed suddenly in a very bad temper. He answered the Barnies gruffly, said that everything was all right now, and any talking could be done tomorrow. As for him, he was going to bed!

The Barnies dispersed at once, still talking. Mr Penruthlan silently led the way back to the farmhouse with Julian and Dick trailing behind. Yan had gone like a shadow. As he wasn't at the farmhouse when they walked wearily into the kitchen, Julian guessed that he'd scampered back up the hills to his grandad.

'Five past three in the morning,' said Mr Penruthlan, looking at the clock. 'I'll sleep down here for an hour or two, then I'll be up to milk the cows. Send these children to bed. I'm too weary to talk. Goodnight.'

And with that he put his hand to his mouth and

solemnly took out his false teeth, putting them into a glass of water on the mantelpiece.

'Oooh – ock,' he said to his wife, and stripped off his wet coat.

Mrs Penruthlan hustled Julian and the rest upstairs. They were almost dropping with exhaustion now. The girls managed to undress, but the two boys flopped on their beds and were asleep in half a second. They didn't stir when the cocks crowed, or when the cow lowed, or even when the wagons of the Barnies came trundling out into the yard to be packed with their things. They were going off to play in another village barn that night.

Julian awoke at last. It took him a few moments to realise why he was still fully dressed. He lay and thought for a while, and a feeling of dejection came over him when he remembered how all the excitement of the day before had ended in complete failure.

If only they knew who had opened that trapdoor! Who could it be?

And then something clicked in his mind, and he knew. Of course! Why hadn't he thought of it before? Why hadn't he remembered to tell Mr

Penruthlan about the Guv'nor standing in the shadows, and his whispered message: 'Here! I'm here!'

He must have been waiting for the smugglers to come to him, of course, he probably used local fishermen to row through the rocks to the motorboat that had slunk over to the Cornish coast, and those fishermen used the Wreckers' Way so that no one knew what they were doing.

The Barnies often came to play at Tremannon Barn. Nothing could be easier than for the Guv'nor to arrange for the smuggling to take place then, for the Wreckers' Way actually had an entrance in the shed near the big barn! If a stormy night came, all the better! No one would be about. He could go up on the hills and wait for the signal from the tower which would tell him that at last the boat was coming.

Yes, and he'd arrange with the signaller too, to flash out the news that he, the Guv'nor, was at Tremannon again, and waiting! Who was the signaller? Probably another of the fishermen, descendants of the old Wreckers, and glad of a bit of excitement.

Everything fell into place, all the odd bits and

pieces of happenings fitted together like a jigsaw puzzle. Julian saw the clear picture.

Who would ever have thought of the owner of the Barnies being involved in smuggling? Smugglers were clever, but the Guv'nor was cleverer than most!

Julian heard the noise outside, and got up to see what it was. When he saw the Barnies piling their furniture on the wagons, he rushed downstairs, yelling to wake Dick as he went. He must tell Mr Penruthlan about the Guv'nor! He must get him arrested! He'd probably got the smuggled goods somewhere in one of the boxes on the wagons. What an easy way of getting it away unseen! The Guv'nor was cunning, there was no doubt about that.

With Dick at his heels, puzzled and surprised, Julian went to find Mr Penruthlan. There he was, watching the Barnies getting ready to go, looking very dour and grim. Julian ran up to him.

'I've remembered something, something important! Can I speak to you?'

They went into a nearby field, and there Julian poured out all he'd guessed about the Guv'nor.

'He was waiting in the dark last night for

the smugglers,' said Julian. 'I'm sure he was. He must have heard us and thought we were the men. And it must have been he who opened the trapdoor. When they didn't come, he must have gone to the trapdoor and found it shut, with things piled on it. And he opened it, and waited there till the men came and handed him the goods. And now he's got them hidden somewhere in those wagons!'

'Why didn't you tell me this last night?' said Mr Penruthlan. 'We may be too late now! I'll have to get the police here to search those wagons, but if I try to stop the Barnies going now, the Guv'nor will suspect something and go off at once!'

Julian was relieved to see that Mr Penruthlan had his teeth in again and could speak properly! The farmer pulled at his black beard and frowned. 'I've searched many times through the Barnies' properties to find the smuggled goods,' he said. 'Each time they've been here I've gone through everything in the dead of night.'

'Do you know what it is they're smuggling?' asked Julian. The farmer nodded.

'Yes. Dangerous drugs. Drugs that are sold at enormously high prices in the black market. The parcel wouldn't need to be very big. I've suspected one or other of the Barnies of being the receivers before this, and I've searched and searched. No good.'

'If it's a small parcel it could be hidden easily,' said Dick, thoughtfully. 'But it's a dangerous thing to hide. The Guv'nor wouldn't have it on him, would he?'

'Oh no, he'd be afraid of being searched,' said Mr Penruthlan. 'Well, I reckon I must let them go this time, and I must warn the police. If they want to search the wagons on the road, they're welcome. I can't get the police here in time to stop the wagons going off. We've got no phone at the farm.'

Mr Binks came up at that moment, carrying Clopper's front and back legs. He grinned at the boys. 'You led us a fine dance last night!' he said. 'What happened?'

'Yes,' said Sid, coming up with Clopper's ridiculous head under his arm as usual. 'Clopper was right worried about you!'

'You didn't carry Clopper's head all over the hills last night, did you?' said Dick, astonished.

'No. I left it with the Guv'nor,' said Sid. 'He

took charge of his precious Clopper while I went gallivanting over the hills and far away, looking for a pack of annoying kids!'

Dick stared at the horse's head, with its comical rolling eyes. He stared at it very hard indeed. And then he did something very strange!

He snatched the head away from the surprised Sid, and raced across the farmyard with it! Julian looked after him in amazement.

Sid gave an angry yell. 'Now then! What do you think you're doing? Bring that horse back at once!'

But Dick didn't. He ran around a corner and disappeared. Sid went after him, and so did somebody else!

The Guv'nor raced across the yard at top speed, looking furious! He shouted, he yelled, he shook his fist. But when he and Sid got to the corner, Dick had disappeared!

'What's got into him?' said Mr Penruthlan, amazed. 'What does he want to rush off with Clopper's head for? The boy must be mad.'

Julian suddenly saw light. He knew why Dick had snatched Clopper's head. He knew!

'Mr Penruthlan, why does the Guv'nor always

have someone in charge of Clopper's head?' he said. 'Maybe he hides something precious there, something he doesn't want anyone to find! Quick, let's go and see!'

19 Mostly about Clopper

At that moment Dick appeared again, around another corner, still holding Clopper's head, with Sid and the Guv'nor hard on his heels. He hadn't been able to stop for a moment, or even to hide anywhere. He panted up to Mr Penruthlan, and thrust the head at him.

'Take it. I bet it's got the goods in it!'

Then Sid and the Guv'nor raced up too, both in a furious rage. The Guv'nor tried to snatch Clopper away from the big farmer. But he was a small man and Mr Penruthlan was well over six feet. He calmly held the horse's head out of reach with his strong right hand, and fended off the Guv'nor with the other.

Everyone ran up at once. The Barnies surrounded the little group in excitement, and one or two farm men came up too. Mrs Penruthlan and the girls, who were now up, heard the excitement and came running out as well. Hens scattered away, clucking, and the four dogs and Timmy barked madly.

The Guv'nor was beside himself with fury. He began to hit the farmer, but was immediately pulled away by Mr Binks.

Then one of the farm men shouldered his way through the excited crowd, and put his great hand on to the Guv'nor's shoulder. He held him in a grip of iron.

'Don't let him go,' said the farmer.

He lowered Clopper's head and looked around at the puzzled Barnies.

'Fetch that barrel,' he said to Julian, and the boy got it at once, placing it in front of the farmer. The Guv'nor watched, his face going white.

'You leave that horse alone,' he said. 'It's my property. What do you think you're doing?'

'You say this horse is your property?' said the farmer. 'Is it entirely your property, inside as well as outside?'

The Guv'nor said nothing. He looked very worried indeed. Mr Penruthlan turned the head upside down, and looked into the neck. He put his hand in and scrabbled about. He found the little lid and opened it. Out fell about a dozen cigarettes.

'They're mine,' said Mr Binks. 'I keep them there. Anything wrong with that, sir? It's a little place the Guv'nor had made for me.'

'Nothing wrong with that, Mr Binks,' said the farmer, and put his hand in again.

He pulled at the lid, and ran his finger around the hole where Mr Binks kept his cigarettes. The Guv'nor watched, breathing quickly.

'I can feel something, Guv'nor,' said Mr Penruthlan, watching the man's face. 'I can feel a false bottom to this clever little space. How do I get it open, Guv'nor? Will you tell me, or do I smash Clopper up to find it?'

'Don't smash him!' said Sid and Mr Binks together.

They turned to the Guv'nor, puzzled.

'What's up?' said Sid. 'We never knew there was a secret about Clopper.'

'There isn't,' said the Guv'nor, stubbornly.

'Ah, I've found the trick!' said Mr Penruthlan, suddenly. 'Now I've got it!'

He worked his fingers about in the space that he'd suddenly hit on, behind the place where Mr

Binks had his cigarettes. He pulled out a package done up in white paper, a small package, but worth many thousands of pounds!

'What's this, Guv'nor?' he asked the white-faced man. 'Is it one of the many packets of drugs you've handled around this coast? Was it because of this secret of yours that you told Sid never to let Clopper out of his sight? Shall I open this packet, Guv'nor, and see what's inside?'

A murmur arose from the Barnies, a murmur of horror. Sid turned fiercely on the Guv'nor. 'You made me guard your horrible drugs, not Clopper! To think I've been helping you all this time, helping a man who's only fit for prison! I'll never work with Clopper again! Never!'

Almost in tears, poor Sid pushed his way through the amazed Barnies and went off by himself. After a few moments Mr Binks followed him.

Mr Penruthlan put the white package into his pocket.

'Lock the Guv'nor up in the small barn,' he ordered. 'And you, Dan, get on your bike and get the police. As for you, Barnies, I don't know rightly what to say. You've lost your Guv'nor, but it's good riddance, I'll tell you that.'

The Barnies stared after the Guv'nor as he was dragged away by two farm men, over to the small barn.

'We never liked him,' said one. 'But he had money to tide us over bad times. Money from smuggling in those wicked drugs! He used us Barnies as a screen for his goings-on. It's good riddance, you're right.'

'We'll manage,' said another Barnie. 'We'll get along. Hey, Sid, come back. Cheer up!'

Sid and Mr Binks came back, looking serious.

'We're not going to use Clopper any more,' said Sid. 'He'll bring us bad luck. We'll get a donkey instead and work up another act. Mr Binks says he couldn't wear Clopper again, and I feel the same.'

'Right,' said the farmer, picking up Clopper's head. 'Get the back and front legs. I'll take charge of Clopper. I've always been fond of him, and he won't bring any bad luck to *me*!'

There was nothing more to be done. The Barnies said rather a sad goodbye. Sid and Mr Binks shook hands solemnly with each of the children. Sid gave Clopper one last pat and turned away.

'We'll go off now,' said Mr Binks. 'Thanks for everything, Mr Penruthlan. Bye!'

'See you again when next you're by here,' said Mr Penruthlan. 'You can have my barn any time, Sid.'

The Guv'nor was safely locked up, waiting for the police. Mr Penruthlan picked Clopper up, legs and all, and looked down at the five children, for Yan was now with them.

He smiled at them all, looking suddenly like a different man.

'Well, that's all finished!' he said. 'Dick, I thought you'd gone mad when you went off with Clopper's head!'

'It was a bit of a brainwave,' said Dick, modestly. 'It came over me all of a sudden. Only just in time, too, the Barnies were nearly on their way again!'

They went over to the farmhouse. Mrs Penruthlan had already run across. The girls guessed why, and they were right!

'I'm getting a meal for you!' she cried, as they came in. 'Poor children, not a mite to eat have you had today. No breakfast, nothing. Come away in and help me. You can turn out the whole larder if you like!'

They very nearly did! Ham and pies went on the table. Anne picked crisp lettuces from the garden and washed them. Julian piled tomatoes in a dish. George cooked a dozen hard-boiled eggs at the stove. A fruit tart and a jam tart appeared as if by magic and two great jugs of creamy milk were set at each end of the table.

Yan hovered around, getting into everybody's way, his eyes nearly falling out of his head at the sight of the food. Mrs Penruthlan laughed.

'Get away from under my feet! Do you want to eat with us?'

'Yes,' said Yan, his eyes sparkling. 'Yes!'

'Then go upstairs and wash those dirty hands!' said the farmer's wife. And, amazingly, Yan went off upstairs as good as gold, and came down with hands that really were almost clean!

They all sat down. Julian solemnly put a chair beside him, and arranged Clopper in such a way that it looked as if he were sitting down too! Anne giggled.

'Oh, Clopper! You look almost real. Mr Penruthlan, what are you going to do with him?'

'I'm going to give him away,' said the farmer, munching as hard with his teeth as he did without them. 'To friends of mine.'

'Lucky friends!' said Dick, helping himself to a hard-boiled egg and salad. 'Do they know how to work the back and front legs, sir?'

'Oh yes,' said the farmer. 'They know fine. They'll do well with Clopper. There's only one thing they don't know. Haw – haw-haw!'

The children looked at him in surprise. Why the sudden laugh?

Mr Penruthlan choked, and his wife banged him on the back. 'Careful now, Mr Penruthlan,' she said. 'Mr Clopper's looking at you!'

The farmer laughed again. Then he looked around at the listening children.

'I was telling you,' he said, 'there's only one thing these friends of mine don't know.'

'What's that?' asked George.

'Well, they don't know how to undo the zip!' said the farmer, and roared again till the tears came into his eyes. 'They don't know how to – how to – haw-haw-haw-haw – undo the ZIP!

'Mr Penruthlan now, behave yourself!' said his amused wife. 'Why don't you say straight out that you're giving Clopper to Julian and Dick, instead of spluttering away like that?'

'Are you really?' said Dick, delighted. 'Thanks so much!'

'Well, you got me what I wanted, so it's only right and fair I should give you what you wanted,' said the farmer, taking another plate of ham. 'You'll do well with Clopper, you and your brother. You can give us a show one day before you leave for home. Haw-haw – Clopper's a funny one, see him looking at us now!'

'He winked!' said George, in an astonished voice, and Timmy came out from under the table to stare at Clopper with the others. 'I saw him wink!'

Well, it wouldn't be surprising if he did wink. He's really had a very exciting time!

THE
FAMOUS FIVE'S
SURVIVAL GUIDE

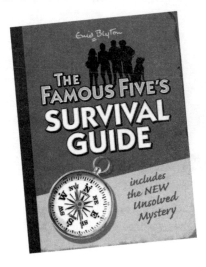

includes
the NEW
Unsolved
Mystery

*Packed with useful information on surviving outdoors and solving
mysteries, here is the one mystery that the Famous Five never managed
to solve. See if you can follow the trail to discover the location of the
priceless Royal Dragon of Siam.*

The perfect book for all fans of mystery, adventure and the Famous Five!

ISBN 9780340970836

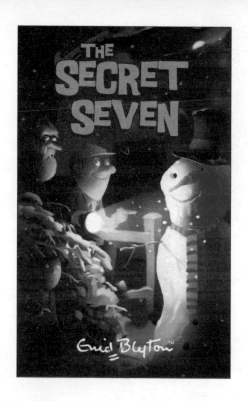

Meet Peter, Janet and Jack, Barbara, Pam, Colin and
George. Together they are The Secret Seven –
ready to solve any mystery, anytime!
A great introduction to adventure stories.

For the full range of Secret Seven books and eBooks, please see
www.hodderchildrens.co.uk

Hodder
Children's
Books

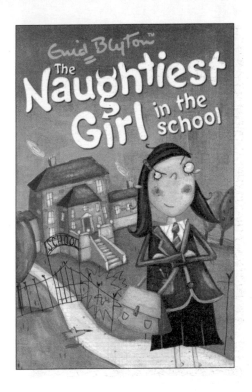

Elizabeth Allen is spoilt, mischievous and determined
to get home – whatever the cost – she really is the
Naughtiest Girl in the school! Exciting stories about
the girls and boys boarding at Whyteleafe School.

Hodder
Children's
Books

THE FAMOUS FIVE ADVENTURE GAME BOOK

Meet the Famous Five and be part of the adventure in these bumper fun game books.

Follow the clues and solve the mystery but watch out for red herrings!

For more fun and games visit
www.famousfivebooks.com

Game Book 1

Game Book 2

9781444900897 £4.99

9781444900903 £4.99

www.famousfivebooks.com

Check out the brand new Famous Five website.

Featuring games and downloads from avatars to screen savers for mobile phones and wallpapers. Enter our amazing monthly competitions and online team challenges to win fab prizes, including limited edition merchandise only available on the website.

www.famousfivebooks.com
www.hodderchildrens.co.uk

The Famous Five

Enid Blyton

Book 1: Five On A Treasure Island

Join Julian and Dick, Anne and George – not forgetting Timmy the dog, in all their exciting adventures!

A shipwreck off Kirrin Island means there must be treasure! The Famous Five can't wait to investigate – but they're not alone. Someone else is treasure-hunting too. Who will follow the clues and get there first?

The Famous Five

Enid Blyton

Book 2: *Five Go Adventuring Again*

Join Julian and Dick, Anne and George – not forgetting Timmy the dog, in all their exciting adventures!

There's a thief at Kirrin Cottage! The intrepid five – Julian, Dick, Anne, George and Timmy are determined to find out who it is, but without any proof, they're stumped. Then they discover a map, and a secret hideaway! All of a sudden, things are falling into place . . .

The Famous Five

Enid Blyton

Book 3: Five Run Away Together

Join Julian and Dick, Anne and George – not forgetting Timmy the dog, in all their exciting adventures!

Who's been on Kirrin Island? When the Famous Five discover a mysterious, locked trunk there, they're suspicious – what can be locked inside it? Just when they think that smugglers are to blame, a chilling scream throws them right off the scent. Things are looking more sinister by the minute . . .

The Famous Five

Enid Blyton

Book 4: *Five Go To Smuggler's Top*

Join Julian and Dick, Anne and George – not forgetting Timmy the dog, in all their exciting adventures!

Staying at Kirrin Cottage, it doesn't take long for Julian, Dick, George and Anne to come across something out of the ordinary. Kirrin Cottage is a rambling, old house, with secret hiding places, and even an underground tunnel. And the Five aren't the only ones to discover them . . . somebody else is using the tunnel, too! But exactly who, and why? It's up to the Famous Five to find the answers . . .

Another Hodder Children's book

The Famous Five

Enid Blyton

Book 5: Five Go Off In A Caravan

Join Julian and Dick, Anne and George – not forgetting Timmy the dog, in all their exciting adventures!

A caravan holiday for the Famous Five! It's bound to be another adventure for the intrepid gang. And sure enough, pretty soon they've caught up with a circus – where some of the circus folk have more sinister plans than just clowning around . . .